RETURN TO THE CASTING COUCH

'You still don't get it do you, Jason? If you want to work in this town, you have to be nice to me. Got it?' There was no room for misunderstanding. It was naked power.

'Yes,' he said.

'Good. That wasn't difficult was it. Now lock the door. watching you has made me horny, Jason. I remember how good you are.'

She reached out her hand and pulled him down to kiss her on the mouth. But she didn't kiss him for long. Hanna was strong and she was soon pushing him down towards the floor.

'Make it good this time as well,' she said, her voice husky with passion but threatening too . . .

Also available from Headline Delta

Amateur Nights
Amateur Days
The Casting Couch
Bianca
Compulsion
Two Weeks in May
The Downfall of Danielle
Exposed
Indecent
Fondle in Flagrante
Fondle on Top
Fondle all Over
Hot Pursuit
Kiss of Death
The Phallus of Osiris
Lust on the Loose
Passion in Paradise
Reluctant Lust
The Wife-Watcher Letters
Amorous Appetites
Hotel D'Amour
Intimate Positions
Ménage à Trois
My Duty, My Desire
Sinderella
The Story of Honey O
Three Women
Total Abandon
Wild Abandon

Return to the Casting Couch

Becky Bell

Copyright © 1995 Becky Bell

The right of Becky Bell to be identified as the Author of
the Work has been asserted by her in accordance with the
Copyright, Designs and Patents Act 1988.

First Published in 1995
by HEADLINE BOOK PUBLISHING

A HEADLINE DELTA paperback

10 9 8 7 6 5 4 3 2 1

All rights reserved. No part of this publication may be
reproduced, stored in a retrieval system, or transmitted,
in any form or by any means without the prior written
permission of the publisher, nor be otherwise circulated
in any form of binding or cover other than that in which
it is published and without a similar condition being
imposed on the subsequent purchaser.

All characters in this publication are fictitious
and any resemblance to real persons, living or dead,
is purely coincidental.

ISBN 0 7472 4688 2

Typeset by Avon Dataset Ltd., Bidford-on-Avon, B50 4JH

Printed and bound in Great Britain by
Cox & Wyman Ltd, Reading, Berks

HEADLINE BOOK PUBLISHING
A division of Hodder Headline PLC
338 Euston Road
London NW1 3BH

Return to the Casting Couch

Chapter One

'So, what do you think, baby? Do you think it's possible?' She stood looking down at him, her big meaty breasts pushing against the prison-issue shirt she had knotted under them, her navel bare. Her thighs were meaty too. She had cut the legs off the prison trousers to form shorts and he could see, at her crotch, a tangle of pubic hair extending out from the ragged edges. 'I mean, you do fancy me, don't you, baby?'

She laughed. The laughter made her breasts quiver. He could see her nipples were erect.

'Don't you?' she prompted, slapping her hand down on his naked thigh so hard it stung him with pain.

He nodded furiously, wanting to avoid a second blow.

'Didn't catch that, baby,' she teased and delivered the second slap anyway, exactly where the first had been but much harder.

He nodded again and tried to pronounce the word 'yes' but the panties stuffed into his mouth and held there by a nylon stocking wrapped around his head and tied tight, didn't allow him to produce more than a muffled groan.

They had stripped him and used nylon tights and stockings to tie him to the big double bed in the master bedroom, pulling the nylon around the legs at each corner, stretching him out, the nylon cutting into his wrists and ankles. The bedroom had been ransacked, the means of his bondage extracted from a chest of drawers, the remains of its contents – bras, panties, and suspender belts, in silk and satin and lace, expensive lingerie from the best designers – strewn across the bedroom floor.

As soon as they had him secured, the five women had drawn lots. Olga had won. It had been four hundred and thirty-two days since she'd had a man. All of the women were lifers. Some had gone much longer than Olga without sex. They would get their turn but she had won the right to go first. She didn't mind if they watched – in fact that's what she wanted.

'So?' Olga repeated. 'You think it's possible?'

He didn't understand the question. He didn't know whether 'yes' was the right answer. He tried to tell her with his eyes that he'd do anything she wanted.

'Answer me, you bastard,' she said slapping her hand down on his other thigh, narrowly missing his cock. 'You think it's possible for a woman to rape a man?' She slapped his thigh again. Both were reddened by her blows.

Now that he understood he nodded vigorously and tried to get the word 'yes' through the silky nylon that filled his mouth, though he wasn't at all sure 'yes' was what she wanted to hear. Nor was he sure it was true. His cock was flaccid, hanging limply between his open thighs. His fear of what the women were going to do to him, especially the leader who had threatened him with a wicked-looking hunting knife to get him to lie on the bed, had kept it that way.

'Oh, so you think so, do you? Well, baby, you're going to have to do a lot better than this . . .' She picked up his cock between her thumb and forefinger, as though it filled her with distaste, then dropped it again, letting it flop back between his legs. 'Isn't that right?' she snapped when he failed to nod his head immediately, reinforcing her point with yet another painful slap, this time aimed at his upper arm stretched out over his head. 'What do you think, girls?'

Two of the other girls were watching, both blondes. In the lottery they had drawn second and third places. Neither had been near a man for three years.

'I think he needs a bit of encouragement,' the one with the longest blonde hair said.

'What, like this?' Olga asked, unknotting the grey shirt and letting her breasts fall free. They were big. He didn't think he'd ever seen bigger – great mounds of flesh, stretched by their own weight and quivering at their newfound freedom, their nipples, small in comparison, surrounded by circles of dark brown areolae. Squashing them between her upper arms Olga shook them from side to side, the flesh making a slapping noise as they hit each other. 'Do you like big tits?' she asked the man.

He nodded.

'Show him the rest,' the other blonde prompted. Both on-lookers had selected items from the ransacked lingerie drawers. The blonde with the long hair wore a black silk teddy, silk so smooth she had never felt anything like it in her life. It was cut so high on the hip that the whole of her flank was exposed. The bra of the garment was cupped in lace allowing glimpses of her breast and nipple. The other girl, her hair cut short, almost cropped, had taken a white suspender belt, white sheer stockings and a white three-quarters-cup bra, which was at least two sizes two small for her, making her breasts balloon out of it obscenely.

No panties covered her blonde pubic hair.

'I'll give him a show, all right,' Olga said. He watched as she turned her back on him and unbuttoned the cut-down trousers, pulling them down her hips and wriggling her backside from side to side like a stripper. As she stooped to pick them from her ankles, he could see the whole slit of her sex buried between her buttocks and covered in a great mass of hair that grew right up into the cleft of her arse – curly, wiry, thick hair. Her buttocks were as big as her breasts, great ovals of flesh trembling as she moved.

'Hell, that's no good,' the long-haired blonde said.

The man's cock had not moved.

'What's the matter, baby? Don't you like big women? I thought you liked big tits...' Olga took one of her breasts in both hands and fed it up to her mouth so her lips could close on her nipple. She took it between her teeth, then pulled her lips back so he could see what she was doing, taking her hands away so her breast hung from her mouth by the nipple. 'Mmm...' she moaned involuntarily, feeling the tingle of pain turn to instant sexual pleasure.

'I like that,' the short-haired blonde said. She had seen Olga do this before. They had shared a cell together – and a great deal more besides...

Olga repeated the delicious torture with the other breast, feeding it in then taking her hands away and allowing it to hang free from the nipple in her teeth, shaking it and feeling new shocks of pain.

'He's not going to be any good to us,' the long-haired blonde said, looking at the man's limp cock.

'I can get him up and keep him up,' the other blonde said, looking at Olga as if for permission, not wanting

RETURN TO THE CASTING COUCH

to be accused of jumping the queue.

'Hey, do it, sister,' Olga said. 'He's no good to any of us like this.'

The blonde searched the clothing strewn around the floor until she found another nylon stocking. She stretched it between her hands until it was like a thin black string.

'Where did the bitch keep her earrings?' she asked.

'Over there.'

The blonde found a jewellery box on the dressing table. She flipped it open, searched briefly, then found what she was looking for.

'Ain't that lucky. She didn't have pierced ears.'

She held up two plain silver earrings, opening their clips as she came back to the bed.

Taking the man's nearest nipple in her finger and thumb she pinched it with her nail then snapped the clip of the earring over it. The man groaned. She did the same thing to the other nipple.

'Doesn't that look pretty?' Olga said.

'That's prettier . . .' the blonde added, pointing to a very discernible movement in the man's cock. Immediately, she dipped her head and sucked the growing erection into her mouth. She didn't lick it or tease it with her tongue, she just devoured it, taking it back into her mouth with all the suction she could create, her cheeks deflated by the effort. The man groaned again, but his cock swelled rapidly in her mouth.

'Yes!' Olga said seeing the shaft swelling between the blonde's lips.

Only when she couldn't hold her breath any longer did she release it, letting it slide from her mouth. She had given birth to a proud throbbing infant. But she hadn't finished yet. Taking the black stocking, she stretched it out again, then ran it down under his balls and up around the top of his shaft, tying it in a slip knot, tightening it. Then she pulled the two ends forward around either side, knotting it again in front before bringing the nylon down between his balls, separating them, then pulling the two ends of the stocking apart again, around the bottom of the shaft and up on top of the first knot where she tied them off securely. It was a neat package, his cock and balls tied up, straining against their constriction. She had tied the nylon tight.

'Jesus, honey, where did you learn that?' Olga asked.

'I was always good with knots.'

'Well, that's going to make things hard for him.'

'And for us.'

They all laughed.

Olga climbed on the bed. After four hundred and thirty-two days she didn't intend to wait any longer. She swung her thigh over the man's hips and immediately felt his cock nuzzling into her thickly haired labia.

'You spunk, honey, and I promise I'll see to it you never come again. Never ever. Got that?'

She looked down at him and he nodded vigorously. The silver earrings bit into his nipples, looking incongruous on his well-developed chest.

Sinking lower, Olga let the cock find its own way between her labia not caring if the curls of her wiry pubic hair scratched his glans. She wriggled until it was touching her clitoris, then she moved ever so slightly so she could feel the hot flesh rubbing against the centre of her sexual nerves. She moaned as she felt the cock pulse, making her clitoris spasm in turn. Moving back she made the cock plough the hairy furrow of her labia until she could feel it right at the mouth of her sex.

Poised there she stopped. She looked at the other two women staring at her, their eyes focused on the shaft sticking upright between her legs, its veins distended with blood trapped by the nylon binding. She knew they were imagining what it would feel like when it came to their turn to have cock again. She could see it in their eyes, the envy and the need.

She could feel the heat of the cock radiating out over her labia. She could feel her own wetness, not just leaking out of her but flooding, streaming down his circumcised glans and on to his balls. She could have come in this position, come just by swaying back and forth, letting it push against her clit, but she had no intention of doing that. All this was teasing – teasing herself, playing with herself, seeing how long it would be before she could stand it no longer, building a dam for her passions which would inevitably burst.

One minute. Two. Thirty seconds more. And that was it, no more. The dam shattered, the water poured through. She dropped herself on to him, right down on to him so he reared up into her body with incredible force. He was big. Very big. She didn't ride him. She didn't pull back and have him pump into her. There was no need. Instead she concentrated every muscle, every effort, every last drop of energy on forcing herself further down on him, down until she could feel him as deep as any man had ever been, down until she could feel his balls, so prominent because of the way they were tied, hot against her arse, down until her body took control and she was shuddering, shaking and trembling, her big breasts smacking into each other, her whole body alive, exploding with feeling, impaled on a cock as hard as a bone.

She didn't leave it there. As soon as she had any control again she started to ride him, bounding up and down on him, exactly like a rider on a horse, pulling herself up on her haunches until the cock was all but out of her, then slamming down on it again, up and down in a blur of motion so fast, so hard, the man moaned pitifully through the panties. She didn't care. The first orgasm had only been preparation for the second, and the second was coming now, coming like an express train as she reamed the helpless cock into her, every stroke increasing the intensity of the final explosion, bringing it closer and closer.

'Yes!' she screamed as she came, still ramming herself up and down on him, still capable of feeling more. Finally, she stopped, exhausted and replete, staying the movement of her breasts by catching them in her hands.

Aftershocks, little orgasms in miniature, rippled through her, delicious reminders of the main event, making her sex throb against the hard cock inside her. Eventually, when they too had gone, she climbed off her victim. His cock was soaking wet, glistening with her juices. The nylon that held it so tightly was soaked too. Her wetness had run down between his legs and he could feel the sheet underneath his buttocks was damp.

'Your turn,' Olga said to the blonde in the white stockings, as she managed to steady herself enough to get off the bed. After so long without a man she was finding it difficult to control her muscles.

'He looks hot,' the blonde said.

The man had sweat running down his forehead. The blonde wiped it away with her hand. She picked up the hunting knife their leader had left on the bedside table. Immediately the man flinched.

'Don't worry. What, you think I don't want my turn?' She laughed, then used the tip of the knife to cut the nylon that held the gag in place. It sliced through it effortlessly. Fishing in his mouth, she extracted the panties. They had been pink but now, soaked with his saliva, they had turned a dark red. She threw them aside. 'You give good head, honey?' she asked stroking his lips with her fingers.

'Yes,' he replied croakily.

'You better, sweet thing, 'cause I'm going to be chewing on your cock till you make me come. So the sooner the better, got it?'

Putting the knife down again she climbed up on the bed kneeling by his face, then swung a leg over his head so she was facing his feet.

'Make it extra specially good . . .' she said. Then she leant forward to gobble his cock into her mouth and, at the same time, sank down on her haunches until her labia made contact with his lips.

He tried to do what she said. It was difficult with no hands to help him. He pushed his tongue out and found her labia. Unlike the other women, the blonde's pubic hair was soft and downy and he had no trouble parting the puffy flesh and finding the lozenge of her clit. He worked it vigorously.

Suddenly she felt his cock spasm. She was doing

what she had said she would do. It felt like she was chewing his cock, using her mouth and lips and tongue and even her teeth on it. It hurt, it stung, it ached but at the same time it was incredibly sexy. She'd make him come. He felt his spunk trying to pump into his shaft, trying to get through the tight nylon with little success.

He tried to concentrate on her, tried to forget his cock. He knew he mustn't come. He stabbed at her clit with his tongue, beating against it with a definite rhythm, then circling it, then nudging it from side to side. He slid his mouth back until he could feel the opening of her sex, then pushed his tongue in there, as far as it would go, until he felt his tendons stretched to the limit. He moved back further, feeling for the rough bud of her anus. He pushed his tongue in there too, penetrating the hard ring of muscle, wriggling up inside and feeling her body react, squirming for more.

Licking the whole furrow of her sex he went back to her clit, as she chewed even harder on his cock. Didn't she know she was making him come? She was supposed to be a professional. She must know he couldn't come. He tongued her clit. Judging from her reactions she liked the little circling movements best so he concentrated on that, hoping it would make her come and she'd stop working on his cock.

He felt her body tense. He felt the muscles in her thighs harden and her labia contract, as though sucking his mouth up into her.

'Jesus . . .' she screamed. She didn't have to act, she didn't have to fake her orgasm. She was melting, melting over his mouth, her whole body reduced to quivering jelly, her juices spraying out of her, almost as though she'd spunked. The vice-like grip of her mouth on his cock went limp.

'Cut! And print. Great, Jason. That was just great, boy. Hey, can we get props? Get him out of this will you...' Len Furey jumped up from his folding canvas director's chair and ran on to the set, as the blonde climbed off the bed. 'Real great, Jason,' Furey repeated.

The props girl picked up the hunting knife and sawed through the nylon stockings that held Jason MacIver to the bed and he sat up, every part of his body aching. She gave him a towel to wipe his face and he ran his fingers through his long blond hair, plucking the earrings from his nipples.

'You nearly made me come, Mandy,' he complained to the blonde.

'Sorry, Jas, I just got carried away. Not surprising considering what you were doing to me. You've got a great move on you...' Mandy ran her hands down Jason's naked body, tracing the outline of the well-developed muscles of his chest and abdomen. 'I mean you're really something...'

'OK, everyone, that's lunch. Then we go straight into the last shot.'

There was a smattering of applause at this from the crew, and the camera was rolled away and lights turned off.

Jason slipped into the white towelling robe the wardrobe assistant handed him, unknotted the nylon tied around his cock and headed for his dressing room at the back of the sound stage. Normally, he had been told, most porno movies were made on the cheap, using the most basic facilities and equipment, but Hollywood Blues Productions were different. On the back of a string of successes and clever marketing, versions of each movie edited to meet the censorship rules of each country, no expense was spared to make films of high quality, in proper studios with all the same production values as a regular feature film. The only difference was that on this film the studio doors were barred and bolted against anyone not involved in the shooting.

Inside his well-appointed dressing room, Jason was soon under the shower, letting the warm water play over his aching limbs. The muscles in his thighs and shoulders ached from being tied to the bed and his neck was sore from straining up to get at Mandy's sex. His cock too was tender where the nylon had cut deep into its engorged flesh, and there were marks on his wrists and ankles.

He was delighted *Escape of the Whores* was almost over. He couldn't pretend it had all been bad. Rolling around in bed with five beautiful women was not exactly a penance, despite the difficulties of having to perform on cue in front of a film camera and crew. In fact, he had always been good at sex and had found a way of using all the people standing around watching as a turn-on; he'd even taken pride in his obvious prowess.

But he had not come to Hollywood to star in porno films. He was an actor, RADA-trained, winner of the gold medal in his year, and he was determined to succeed as a straight actor. The circumstances that had led him to appearing in *Escape of the Whores* had been beyond his control and he had simply had no choice. Well, he told himself constantly, he had at least managed to stay in Hollywood and had gained experience of making a film, however bizarre. If it had not been for the offer from Len Furey, he would have had to return to England penniless and with his tail between his legs. The money from the film had given him a breathing space. Now the film was almost over he could devote his time to trying to get his legitimate career back on track.

Drying himself quickly and combing his hair, Jason glanced at his naked body in the big full-length mirror that lined the dressing-room door. The Los Angeles sun had given him a nice even tan and his regular workouts kept his muscles firm and well defined, adding to the impression of strength that his height produced. His blue eyes stared back at him with amusement – he had not lost his sense of humour, despite the difficulties life in general, and Hanna Silverstein in particular, had thrown at him.

He stepped into a pair of white cotton boxer shorts and pulled on his jeans. Remarkably, the marks on his wrists and ankles were already beginning to fade.

There was a knock on the dressing room door.

'Come in,'

'Hi!' It was Mandy. She was wearing a peach-coloured satin robe that clashed with her straw-coloured short-cropped blond hair. It was obvious she was naked under the robe. 'I came to apologise.'

'For what?' he asked, though he knew the answer.

'For getting carried away.'

'Forget it.'

'Len would have been mad with me if I'd made you come. He'd have had to put off the shot this afternoon and all . . .'

'You didn't.'

'It's just that... well, what you were doing...'

'Forget it,' he repeated.

'I wish I could.'

She looked at him wistfully as he pulled his denim shirt on. Over the last four weeks she had seen his body in every conceivable position, watched him as he was fucked and sucked and manipulated by the four other actresses, watched as he fucked and sucked and manipulated her.

'You just get to me, Jas...' She put her hand out and touched his cheek.

'Look, Mandy...' he started to say.

'I know, I know... It's cool. You don't want me. I know that. You've got more women chasing you than a bitch on heat. What do you need me for? I ain't no Camilla Potts. I just came to tell you I've done six of these pieces of shit before and I never came on camera once. I always had to fake it. But with you... Jesus! You practically only have to look at me. There's just something about you, Jas. The way you move... I don't know... Anyway I'm finished now so I'm off.' She took a little card from the pocket of the robe. It had numbers scrawled over it in very childish writing. 'Just in case you ever feel like coming down market...'

Mandy put the card down on the dressing table, untied the belt of the robe so it opened to reveal her naked body, took one step forward, caught both Jason's cheeks in her hands and kissed him full on the mouth, rubbing her breasts against his chest and squirming her thigh up between his legs.

'Oh, sorry...' Camilla Potts hadn't bothered to knock. She stood in the doorway.

'Don't worry,' Mandy said coolly, 'I was just saying

goodbye.' She unravelled herself from Jason's body and pulled the robe around her body again.

'Not on my account, please,' Camilla said with an amused expression.

'Just can't get enough of him, that's my problem,' Mandy said honestly as she left. 'Bye, lover.'

'Bye,' Jason said lamely.

Camilla closed the door after her.

'I didn't interrupt, did I?'

'She was just saying goodbye apparently.'

Camilla laughed. 'Are you coming to lunch?'

As usual Camilla Potts looked stunning. More often than not she dressed herself in clinging shiny Lycra, leggings and leotard or all-in-one catsuits, the material clinging to every curve of her incredibly curvaceous body – her firm up-tilted breasts, her slim waspie waist, her iron-flat stomach and pert round buttocks, the slender contours of her long, long legs. Today the Lycra was yellow, a catsuit so tight that, as she stood with her legs together, Jason could see a clear gap at the top of her thighs, immediately under the bulge of her sex – a roughly diamond-shaped gap that seemed to invite attention.

Jason looked into her soft brown eyes. Her brunette hair was cut short, emphasising her long neck and fine almost aristocratic features – high cheekbones, a very straight nose and symmetrical mouth, with rather thin lips. Camilla Potts could easily have been a member of one of the older American families from New England, a member of what passed for American nobility; instead she was America's leading pornographic movie star.

They walked to the commissary together arm in arm. It had been through Camilla that Jason had become involved with Len Furey and *Escape of the Whores* and, though he would rather have been given the job he'd been promised – the promise that had brought him to LA in the first place – he was grateful to her for helping him out of the awkward situation he had found himself in. He also had to admit that she was one of the most beautiful women he had ever seen. It had not been difficult 'acting' with her over the last few weeks – if having sex with her on camera could be called acting, especially as they had already established a sexual rapport off set.

There was a pirate picture being made on the next sound stage and the commissary was full of actors in seventeenth-century costumes, big leather boots with doublet and hose. They found an empty table among the throng, then queued up for a salad and a bottle of Evian.

'Len says he's really pleased with you,' Camilla volunteered as she toyed with a lettuce leaf.

'Is he?' Jason said with no enthusiasm.

'Sure. I mean, like this morning. That's not easy to do.'

'You were watching? I didn't see you.'

'That's hardly surprising. You don't mind, do you?'

'Why should I mind?'

'They normally have to take a whole day over a scene like that. Ice the guy's cock down so he can't get it up, then spend all afternoon warming it up again. You did it in one take.'

'No wonder Len's pleased.'

'How do you do it?'

'What?'

'Keep it soft. I mean with all those women around.'

'Oh, I just thought about what Hanna Silverstein did to me.'

Camilla laughed. 'Right... easy then.'

'That's enough to turn anyone off.'

'Don't worry about it. When she sees you in this she'll change her mind.'

'You think so?' Jason looked optimistic.

'Sure. You're great. I mean you act great, not just the fucking.'

'Really?'

'Sure. Jason, you're going to make it big. We both are. If Len can get the money for his straight film we'll both make it big. You see. And he'll get it. It might take time but he'll get it. Len's one of the good guys.'

'I hope so.'

'Trust me. It's a great script. It's got a great part for you and a great part for me. Everyone who reads it thinks it's the best thing since pepper in salami.'

'Why won't they finance it then?'

'Politics. There's a lot of politics in this town. He'll get the money in the end. Trust me.'

'I do.'

The truth was, of course, that he had little choice.

'Speed,' Len Furey shouted.

'Speed,' the cameraman confirmed.

'Right. Action.'

'Untie my hands, please...' Jason said.

'I can't,' Camilla replied.

'Why not?'

They were lying on the bed in the ransacked bedroom.

'Be quiet, you'll wake the others. They're only next door.'

Jason's hands were tied behind his back with a leather strap. His cock was buried to the hilt in Camilla's hairless sex. She had hauled him up on top of her and pushed his cock down between her legs. The camera had moved in for a close-up as her hand guided it to the mouth of her sex and it disappeared inside.

'Let me fuck you properly, let me use my hands.'

'Do it like this.'

'Don't you want more? I can give you so much more if you let me. Please...' Jason was acting. His character had seen the chance to escape from the clutches of the women. Their leader was infatuated with him. If he could persuade her to release him he would have a chance to overpower her and be free.

'I can't.'

'Don't you trust me? You know I want you. Please let me fuck you properly. I want it so bad.' He slammed his cock into her with all his might, up and down like a piston, making her moan. 'I know you want it too.'

'No... no...' she said, her body contradicting her words, pulsing in response to his energy.

'You love it.'

'Yes...'

'I can make it better. It's not just sex any more. You know that. You know how I feel about you.'

'Oh, oh...' He was still stabbing his big hard cock into her, arching himself into her as far as he could, working his hips back and forth.

'Come on...'

'Wait...' she said, making up her mind, trying to stop his thrusting so she could think. 'You promise not to tell the others? If they found out they'd kill me.'

'Yes, yes...'

Without saying anything she unbuckled the strap that held his wrists together.

'Yes...' he said, kissing her neck where its tendons were most stretched and making her arch up off the bed involuntarily.

'Let me concentrate...' she chided.

'You are so beautiful. I want to fuck you. I want to spunk you. I want to spunk your cunt...'

'Oh...' The words made her sex throb. Her fingers worked frantically to free the buckle, her eyes wild with passion. 'There...' she said triumphantly as the belt dropped away. For the first time since the five women had invaded the house he was free. He wanted to leap off her and run away but he knew he wouldn't get far. She would raise the alarm and they'd catch him before he got to the front door. He had to be more subtle.

'Darling...' he said, kissing her full on the mouth, one hand working between their bodies to find her clitoris while the other groped for her nipples.

'Oh, oh...' she moaned as his cock bucked into her with renewed vigour. She could feel herself contracting around the bone hardness of his shaft as her orgasm began to build. 'Oh yes...'

He worked like a demon, pumping fast and furious, manipulating her clit at the same time, wanting her to come hard, wanting to plunge her into such ecstasy she wouldn't have any senses left to cope with what he planned.

'You want it?' he demanded huskily. 'You want my spunk?'

'Yes, yes, give it to me...'

His spunk would be the last straw. To feel his cock kicking and jerking in the tight confines of her sex, his white-hot spunk jetting out into the very centre of her, would be more than she could bear. She felt him tense, felt his whole body go rigid, but before she could feel anything else, her own orgasm overtook her. Her body started to tremble and she was thrown down a vertical precipice into a pit of darkness and absolute pleasure, falling ever deeper.

Somewhere in the pit, she felt him turning her over. He wanted to take her from behind. She didn't protest. She was too far gone to do anything. His hands pulled her on to her stomach, his hands were moving her wrists, wrapping something around them behind her back...

'What the...' she said, suddenly aware of the danger. But it was too late. Before she could struggle he sat firmly on her back and pushed a pair of panties into her mouth. Quickly he wound a stocking around her head to secure them. He'd got her. He smiled victoriously. Levering himself down until he was sitting on her legs, he wound another stocking around her ankles, like the one he had used on her wrists. He'd got her now.

He climbed off the bed and listened. There was not another sound in the house. The other women were all still sleeping, used to the sound of sex from the next room.

As quietly as he could, he looked for his clothes among the lingerie strewn on the floor. He found jeans and a T-shirt.

He looked at the bound figure as he pulled on the shirt. God, she was beautiful. She was struggling, the movement only making the knots of the nylon tighter. The curves of her round tanned arse were bobbing up and down, her breasts squirming against the sheets.

He felt his cock throb, still erect.

He came closer to the bed looking down at her. She sensed what he was doing and twisted her head around to look up at him, her soft brown eyes full of expression, but it was not anger or hatred that he had cheated her. It was passion, it was unadulterated and unmistakable lust. She could feel his cock as though it were still inside her, like the impression of a key left in soft soap. She could feel her juices running out of her sex, squeezed between her thighs. She begged him, begged him with her eyes to take her again, just one more time.

And he did. He couldn't resist. He fell on her like a hungry wolf, his cock already full of spunk, his need too urgent to ignore in the face of her desire. His shaft slipped between her buttocks and up into her soaking wet sex, despite the fact she couldn't open her legs.

She felt so good, so hot. He took up a rhythm, pounding into her, her buttocks slapping against his navel. She moaned through the panties, a moan of pure pleasure. He didn't care. He wasn't interested in her pleasure, he was too far gone to care about anything but his own. He reamed into her faster, every stroke, every long travail of her hot silky wet sex a provocation, driving him closer and closer to the point where he would have to come, where he would be beyond the point of no control.

'I can't leave you ... I want you. I can't leave you here,' he said. 'We'll go together.' He realised that was what he wanted. He couldn't bear to be parted from her, from this incredible body.

She nodded wildly in agreement.

Their faces registered it all. There was no need for Len Furey to interrupt. They'd got everything perfectly, just as it was written in the script.

Jason pulled out just in time, his control stretched to the limit. The camera closed in quickly. He waited for the sign that the cameraman was ready, his cock throbbing visibly. The cameraman made a circle with his finger and thumb. Immediately Jason ploughed his cock into the cleft of Camilla's pert arse, as she, in turn, arched it up towards him. As he felt his spunk begin to jet out, he pulled his cock away from her body so great big gobs of white-hot spunk shot out over her arse and back, the white in stark contrast to her tanned flesh, easy for the camera to pick out.

The camera focused on a close-up of Jason's hand untying the nylon that held the gag in place, going in tighter as his mouth kissed Camilla on the lips, their tongues vying for position, the kiss long and passionate.

'Cut! Print. Check the gate.'

There was a long pause while the cameraman checked his camera to see if there had been any obstruction on the lens. Satisfied there hadn't been, he nodded to Len.

'And that's a wrap, ladies and gentlemen. There will be drinks on the set in thirty minutes and you're all invited. Thank you for all your efforts . . .'

Applause broke out on the set as technicians began to pack up equipment and turn off lighting. No one seemed to take any notice of Camilla and Jason, still kissing a long time after the camera had ceased to roll.

RETURN TO THE CASTING COUCH

'We'd better go,' Jason said.
'Come to my dressing room...'
'I need to shower...'
'No, let me lick you clean...'

Chapter Two

'Great. Just great!'

The projection screen went blank, flickered then turned white just seconds before the lights came up. In the small viewing theatre racked with three rows of comfortable armchair-like seats with a central console in the middle that communicated directly to the projection box, Hanna Silverstein was sitting with Len Furey on the back row. Jason sat at the front.

As usual Hanna was wearing white – a white Ferragamo suit with big chunky gold buttons, its jacket revealing her rather over-tanned clavicle and the fact that she had small breasts. Her bejewelled fingers played with a thick gold chain that hung around her neck. Hanna was over-thin too, her face often, as now, etched with the burdens of power. Strangely enough though, perhaps because of her soft, beautifully cut blonde hair, Hanna looked younger than her age, most people guessing she was no more than forty.

'You like it?' Len Furey asked.

'I said, it's great. Your best yet. Going to be big.' Hanna replied.

'Yeah, that's what I think. I mean this is only the first cut...'

'Sure, sure...' Hanna was looking at Jason. 'Len, do me a favour would you?'

'Anything.'

'Give me a minute with Jason.'

'Sure thing.'

Len got to his feet rapidly and walked along the back to the door marked with a green EXIT light. Jason thought he detected a knowing look on his face. Whether he did or not, he knew there was no way Len was going to refuse any request Hanna Silverstein made. If she had asked him to lick the soles of her white high-heeled shoes he would have done it. One thing Jason had learnt in Hollywood was that power was treated with total respect and obeisance, and Hanna Silverstein was a very powerful woman.

'Stirs the memory,' Hanna said as the door closed itself on hydraulic hinges, making a slight hissing sound.

'I'd think I'd better go.'

'Don't do that, Jason. There's no hurry is there? I mean you don't have another job to go to, do you?'

'You know damn well I don't,' Jason couldn't keep the anger out of his voice.

'Don't get yourself so het up. You fucked me about. I had to teach you a lesson. That's over now. We can still be friends, can't we?'

'What about *The Casting Couch*?' *The Casting Couch* was the film Hanna had brought Jason to Hollywood for, supposedly to star in. But instead, she had used him as her personal stud, shared him out among her friends, always stalling questions about the film, until one day he had discovered she was auditioning other actors for the part. She had sworn it was necessary to prove they had looked at other American actors before they'd brought in someone from England – a device to get his work permit – but had been so angry that he had dared to question her that she had quite literally thrown him out on the street. He still didn't know the truth: whether he'd been brought over as an attractive stud or whether she genuinely was going to give him the part in the film. Perhaps now he would never know.

'So, are you going to be nice to me?' she said, ignoring his question.

Jason debated what to do. It had been a revelation to him when he had discovered that not only was Hanna Silverstein responsible for a string of Oscar-winning films, she was also making extremely popular porno movies distributed all over the world and transferred to video, netting untold fortunes. She had had him shut out of straight films as part of her revenge but had allowed him to star in *Escape of the Whores*, a production which, Jason had discovered, she was backing.

'I think I should go,' he said hesitantly.

'I think you should stay.' Her voice was cold and hard. 'You still don't get it do you, Jason? You still haven't cottoned on. So why don't I explain it to you in words of one syllable? If you want to work in this town, if you want to live in this town, you have to be nice to me. I had your arse kicked once. I had you blacklisted. I even got your agent to drop you. I gave you a second chance with this shit, which was really good of me. You did good, real good. Don't give me any problems and I may even give you another chance. May. Got it? May. No promises. Okay?'

There was no room for misunderstanding. It was naked power.

'Yes.'

He wanted to ask if he was still in the running for *The Casting Couch*, which he knew had been postponed, but decided to keep quiet.

'Good. You see that wasn't difficult was it . . .' Her voice was soft and conciliatory. 'Lock the door.'

Trying not to show his reluctance Jason got up, climbed the steps to the door and shot the small metal bolt on the inside.

'You've made me horny, Jason, watching that cock of yours. You're so good with it, aren't you? I remember how good you are . . . and good with your mouth, very good with your mouth too . . .'

She was sitting in the armchair by the central aisle. She reached out her hand and pulled him down to kiss her on the mouth. But she didn't kiss him for long. Instead she took his head in her hands and pushed it down on to her breasts, fumbling with the buttons of the jacket to get it undone. There was no blouse underneath but, despite the fact her breasts were small, she was wearing a white lace bra. Jason could see her nipples poking out through the thin material. She pushed his mouth on to her left breast and he sucked on the nipple through the lace. Hanna moaned.

'Go down on me, Jason. Give me what you gave Mandy . . . That was a great scene . . .'

Despite her appearance, thin and slight, Hanna was strong. Her fingers were like steel, digging into Jason's shoulders and pushing him down to the floor. There was just enough room for him to kneel between the rows of seats. Hanna wriggled the white skirt of the suit up over her thighs and around her hips. She was in too much of a hurry to take it off. She was not wearing tights, only small white lacy panties that matched her bra.

Jason stared into her crotch. Hanna hoisted one leg

after the other over his shoulders, her shoes digging into his back, levering her sex up at him.

'Make it good,' she said her voice husky with passion but threatening too.

He lowered his head as she opened her thighs wider. He could see her very sparse pubic hair through the silky nylon of her panties. Her bony fingers were on the back of his head, pushing him down as she arched her buttocks up off the seat and dug her heels into his back. He kissed her nether lips through the lacy gauze and felt her shudder immediately. The material was already damp and he could taste her juices on it.

Moving his hand up under her thighs, he managed to work his fingertips up to the leg of the panties and pull them aside. He plunged his mouth back on to her sex, his hot tongue finding her clitoris with no difficulty, remembering how he had done it before.

'Yes . . .' Hanna cried out loudly.

He tongued it hard, his anger at the way she was treating him again not allowing him to be subtle or gentle. He used the tip of his tongue like a little hammer, beating a tattoo on her clit.

'Good, good . . .' she cried. 'Oh, Jason . . .'

Then he changed his tactics, pushing his mouth down until he could get his tongue into the wet, sticky tunnel of her sex. He pushed it up as far as it would go, tasting the sap of her body, feeling the walls of her cunt throbbing, his tongue stretched painfully against the tendons that held in it place. He would have liked to have tongued her arse too but in this position it was impossible. Instead he moved his tongue around the opening of her sex, licking it, nudging it. He moved his fingers forward and, as he took his tongue away, slid two fingers as deep as they would go inside her, while his mouth found her clitoris again.

He could feel her coming. Her body was trembling in time to the tempo of his tongue on her clit. She was moaning continuously, repeating over and over again what sounded like 'do it, do it', until her words were meaningless. Every time she repeated them they were louder, until she was screaming, the sound reverberating off the walls of the soundproof screening room.

Suddenly he felt her sex contracting on his fingers, sucking them up into her, her body convulsing.

'Do it,' she screamed one last time at the top of her voice, her whole body rigid as his tongue tapped her clitoris and her orgasm took over, flooding her with feeling, washing away everything but its own existence.

Slowly her body slackened. But she was not finished. The orgasm on his mouth had only created another need, just as urgent as the first.

'Fuck me,' she said, pushing Jason back against the seats of the row in front. She swung her legs off his shoulders and turned round so she was kneeling on the seat of the big armchair, her slender buttocks sticking out, still covered in a silky white triangle of lace and the tail of her jacket.

Jason was wearing jeans and a T-shirt. He unzipped the jeans and began pulling them off.

'Now, Jason. Now ...' Hanna demanded as she looked over her shoulder. The jeans were around his thighs, his cock – the cock she had just seen in big close-up, fucking and buggering five women, singly and together, the cock that had thrilled her so many times – was sticking out fully erect from the fly of his white boxer shorts. She flipped the tail of the jacket up with her hand and wriggled her bottom from side to side impatiently.

There was no point arguing. What Hanna Silverstein wanted, Hanna Silverstein got. Perhaps, if he'd realised that earlier when he'd first come to Hollywood with her, he might not be in the position he was in today, Jason thought. But at least he knew now. He knew the game he had to play and all the rules. Somewhere in the back of his mind he thought there was a chance he could get back into *The Casting Couch*. That could be what she had meant when she said she'd give him a second chance. He would do anything for that.

He caressed her buttocks briefly – hard firm buttocks with very little fat – then pulled her panties down. As soon as her sex was exposed, leaving the white panties around her thighs, he knelt on the seat of the big chair and pushed his cock down between her legs. His saliva and her juices had mixed to make her very wet. She was hot too.

'Fuck me,' she said, wriggling back on him at the first contact. Almost accidentally the movement made his cock slip into her cunt, right up inside her. 'Yes!' she said triumphantly.

He started ramming into her, his hands holding her tightly by the hips. As he pushed forward she pushed back. Her sex was tight and silky. He was in her so deep he could feel the top of her womb against his glans. He knew she was coming again instantly. He could feel her sex contracting rhythmically, gripping his shaft as he reached the deepest point.

'Spunk, spunk . . .' she demanded, without looking

back at him. 'I want it . . . I need it . . .'

He reamed her harder. He was erect but he wasn't turned on. He didn't feel like spunking. The way she was treating him – like a stud, like a piece of meat, like something to be used then discarded – had made him angry. She was using him again, using him like she had used him so many times before.

'Spunk . . .' she cried sensing his reluctance and thrusting back at him.

But Jason knew the rules now. What Hanna Silverstein wanted Hanna Silverstein got. It was as simple as that. He'd give her what she wanted for the sake of another chance.

He slowed the rhythm of his penetrations. He had to get himself to come, to stop thinking about how Hanna was using him, about his career. He remembered the scene she had mentioned, the scene with him tied to the bed and Mandy sitting on his face, her wet labia dripping into his mouth. He remembered how she had gobbled up his cock and how much he'd wanted to come. He couldn't because he had to save himself, save himself for spunking over Camilla's buttocks in the final shot of the film, but he remembered how close he had been. Mandy's mouth had been so hot, so wet, so artful. She'd made it feel like an articulate cunt.

He felt his cock throb, spunk pumping out of his balls.

'Yes . . .' Hanna cried feeling it too.

If he concentrated hard he could feel it again, how Mandy's mouth had sucked on him, chewed his cock, pushed it right back into her throat, how she had licked it on the outward stroke pushing her tongue down into the little slit of his urethra, then gobbled him right up again until he could feel her lips grazing his pubic hair.

'Spunk...' Hanna demanded her body poised, wanting to feel the throes of his orgasm inside her. She could have come again without it, come on the pounding he was giving her but she wanted his spunk, wanted it because it represented her power over him, and power – that sort of power – turned her on.

His cock was throbbing wildly now. He was coming. He'd give her what she wanted. His mind wandered from Mandy to Camilla, remembering when he'd first met her, how she'd stood naked and proud in a mirrored bathroom, her legs open, her completely hairless sex revealing every detail of her labia as she'd stooped to pull on a pair of silk French knickers.

Jason opened his eyes and watched his cock poking through the fly of his boxer shorts – now soaked with Hanna's juices. He pummelled into her bony, sharp, almost pointed arse and felt a huge pulse of sensation rolling up from his cock to the nerves in the back of his eyes, closing them tight shut as his spunk jetted out of his cock and into the tight confines of Hanna's silky, spongy sex.

As Hanna felt his cock spasm, kicking out his seed into her, she felt his convulsions and the flood of his spunk push her over the edge. Her first orgasm still lingered in her nerves, and now this second one joined it, the two together taking her higher, making her float, her mind wallowing in pleasure, the pleasure of sex and the pleasure of power, of the force of will that had got her what she wanted.

The moment passed. She did not move, letting Jason's cock slip out of her naturally, expelled by the inward pressure of her sex.

'OK. You can go now,' she said, being deliberately cold, wanting him to know this was only one act of expiation, that he was not forgiven and would have to do more to get back into her good books.

'What?' he said.

'Just get out, Jason. I'll see you some other time.'

'I thought...' Actually he had no idea what he'd thought would happen after she'd used him. Did he think she was going to invite him back to her house again?

'I don't care what you thought, Jason. Just go. I'll call you. Maybe. Remember no promises...'

Jason pulled up his jeans, combed his hair with his fingers, and, as Hanna pulled her panties back around her hips, he unbolted the door and left without another word. He hated himself for not telling her she couldn't just use him like this, that he was a person, not just a stud, that he had feelings and emotions too. But at the same time, he told himself he had done the right thing, performed for her, done what she required of him, and that that might have gone some way towards a second chance. She wouldn't have considered doing this with him if she wasn't still thinking about him for *The Casting Couch* would she? But that happy thought was soon dispelled. She probably had no intention of helping him at all, she had just been aroused by what she'd seen on film, remembering what it had been like with him and wanting instant gratification. She was playing with him like a cat with a mouse.

Jason walked down the long corridors of the studio – the walls hung with countless stills from the films that had been made on the sound stages – feeling thoroughly depressed. On one side, the walls were glass above waist level, so it was possible to see into the offices and as he passed the suite where Len Furey was based, he saw the director beckoning him in.

'You want me?' he said, opening the office door.

'Sure. Come in. You look as though you need a drink.' Len poured two glasses of bourbon from a bottle on top of a small grey filing cabinet. He handed one to Jason, sipped at the other, and sat behind his desk. 'Command performance?'

'Something like that.'

'You did the right thing, kid.'

'Did I?'

'We've all done it. That's Hollywood.'

'I'm not sure I like Hollywood.'

'Wise up, kid. What's so terrible? So you got laid. What's wrong with that. Plenty of guys who'd swap places with you. And if it helps you get on . . . Cheers.'

'Cheers.' Jason drank a large swig of the bourbon. It made him feel better, or was it that what Len said made sense? 'I suppose you're right.'

'Listen. You're good. Take it from me. I mean not just at the sex. You're good at that certainly, but you're also a good actor. You look good on screen. You've got a presence. You're going to make it. Take it from me.'

'Really?'

'No bullshit. If I can get the money for my film with you in the lead you'll be the hottest thing in this town since Marilyn Monroe's panties.'

'You think you can?'

'Sure. I'm following some good leads.'

'Is there anything I can do?'

'You know anyone who runs a studio?'

He knew Bill Talbot. But like everyone else in

Hollywood that he'd met through Hanna Silverstein, he imagined Bill Talbot would be unlikely to welcome a call from him.

'If I think of anyone I'll let you know.'

'Don't worry. I'll get it. Just keep in touch.'

'Like a limpet.' Jason said, his mood slightly improved.

'Great. It's just great, Jason.'

Nancy Dockery hugged Jason and kissed his cheek. They had had a giant pizza delivered and ate it together on the sofa with a bottle of Californian Cardonnay, watching a rough cut video transfer of *Escape of the Whores* that Len Furey had sent over that morning. Nancy was something of a connoisseur of blue movies, having confessed to Jason on the first night they'd met that she collected them.

'I tell you, Jason. I mean not just the screwing. It's really good. You're really good ... It's going to sell a lot of copies ...'

'That's not good news.' Jason thought the fewer people saw it the better.

'No. Lots of actors started doing this stuff. Success is success in this town. It doesn't matter in what. If you're in a top-grossing skin flick what matters is it's top-grossing. No one cares about anything else. Take my word for it. And you make a real impact.'

'You think so?'

'I know so. Len thinks you're great, doesn't he? He still wants you to do this thriller?'

'He says so all the time.'

'So there you are. When he gets the money for that, you'll make it big. It's a great script, bound to be commercial. You look so good on screen. The camera loves you, Jason...'

'But he still hasn't raised the money.'

'He will.'

'When? It's been months.'

'It takes time.'

'If it's such a good movie, if everyone thinks it's so great why don't they put up the money?'

'Politics. That's Hollywood.'

Jason laughed bitterly. 'God, I've heard that expression so often. It's supposed to explain everything.'

Nancy picked up her glass from the coffee table in front of them and handed Jason his.

'A toast. To Jason MacIver.'

She clinked her glass against his.

'Thanks, Nancy. Thanks for everything.' He looked at her as she sipped her wine. If it hadn't been for Nancy he would have literally been walking the streets after Hanna had had him thrown out of her house. He had told her everything. She was honest and open and took Jason for what he was – a ship that passed in the night. As their relationship had developed, she seemed happy to settle for being with him in the present tense, enjoying his company and not asking for any commitment. Nor, she had made it abundantly clear, did she expect him to remain faithful to her.

She was a beautiful woman. After her shower when she got back from work, she had slipped into a white towelling robe, pinning her long, very black hair, up on her head. Her body was large though not fat, her curves rich and ripe – it was the sort of body a man could drown in. She had the deepest darkest brown eyes he thought he had ever seen and an opulent mouth, its fleshy lips a natural ruby red.

'Watching you and Camilla makes me hot, Jason,' she said looking straight into his eyes.

'You'd better take that robe off then,' he joked.

'I've got a better idea.' She leant forward and kissed his cheeks lightly on both sides. 'Why don't I go and get into something a little more uncomfortable? Give me fives minutes.' She ran her hand up his leg and pinched his cock through his jeans before she got to her feet, pulled the video tape out of the video recorder and disappeared into her bedroom.

Jason sipped his wine, his mind drifting from the glories of Nancy's body to the problems of his career. Since the viewing with Hanna Silverstein, he had hoped she might call him. But she hadn't and neither of his two calls to her – intercepted by a secretary – had been returned. In the best of all possible worlds he had imagined that seeing him in *Escape of the Whores* might have made her put up the money for Len Furey's thriller, with the starring part for him, or that at least she would give him the lead in *The Casting Couch* again, or, better still, both. Instead it appeared to have done neither, apparently not even provoking a desire to have a reprise of their physical encounter.

From the bedroom he heard the introductory music to *Escape of the Whores*. Then he heard the tape being wound forward. Nancy was looking for a particular scene, the one she had found specially exciting, or so she'd told him. He heard the tape stop and the sound of his own voice, though he couldn't hear what he was saying.

'Come to bed, Jason,' Nancy shouted.

He got to his feet and finished his wine, his cock already stirring in anticipation of the delights of Nancy's body and her sensuous touch. Slowly he pushed the bedroom door open. The room was small, dominated by a big brass bedstead. The pine wardrobe and chest of drawers were too large for the room really, both so full of clothes, they did not close properly. The quilted counterpane lay discarded on the floor. On top of the chest of drawers was a television and video recorder. Shelves to one side stored Nancy's collection of porn. She had dimmed the lights so most of the illumination was coming from the television screen, where, in close-up, the mouth of Camilla Potts was closing in on Jason's erection.

With difficulty, always fascinated by the comparatively new experience of seeing himself on screen, Jason tore his eyes from the television to look at Nancy.

'Come and watch me,' she said.

She was lying on the white sheets of the bed, her long legs clad in very sheer and shimmery black stockings, the shine on them making them look as though they were wet, their much darker black welts attached to black satin suspenders, which pulled them into tight chevrons on her creamy thighs. Her legs were open, open so wide that even though the furrow of her sex was covered in abundant, coarse, black curls of pubic hair growing untrimmed in all directions, he could actually see the mouth of her vagina, its folds parted, its dark interior already glistening wet.

Jason pulled off his shirt and took off his shoes and socks, pulling his trousers and pants down together. His cock escaped its constriction, springing up at right angles to his body, the very same cock that now dominated the television screen, being wanked aggressively by Camilla Potts' fine slim fingers.

Nancy looked from one to the other. Her finger, just the very tip of her forefinger, teased out her clitoris from behind her labia, rubbing it in tiny little circles, her own juices making the contact almost frictionless.

'Lovely cock...' she said. 'Just look at that...'

But even the fascination of his own performance could not make him take his eyes off Nancy. She had bent her legs at the knee and was touching herself much harder now, pushing her finger down on the swollen, throbbing lozenge of her clit, while her free hand grabbed at her left breast. Her breasts were big, full and meaty, great cushions of flesh rising from her chest like crested waves. Her hand kneaded the wave, her fingers sinking deep into the spongy meat, pushing it one way, pulling another.

She reached over to the bedside table. There was a bottle of body oil standing ready. Flicking off its cap she poured the oil into the channel of her cleavage, replacing the bottle on the table. Using both her hands, her eyes back on the television screen, she massaged the oil up to her breasts, smoothing it in with the palms of her hands, until her skin glistened. A little of the oil had run down into the dimpled hollow of her navel where it had pooled. Leaving one hand to alternate between her breasts, kneading one then the other, the oil making them deliciously slippery and sensual, she snaked her other hand down her body and back to her clitoris.

'Aren't you going to watch yourself?' she asked.

'I'd rather watch you.'

'That's what I hoped you'd say. Come here where I can reach you.'

He knelt up on the bed by her side. Leaving her breasts she hooked an oily hand around his cock.

'Jesus, you look so sexy,' she said. Since her eyes were on the television, he guessed she meant on screen.

He glanced up to see what she was watching. He remembered the scene. It had been very uncomfortable. The escaped prisoners had decided they wanted sun to get rid of their prison pallor. Since the garden of the house they'd taken over was completely secluded they had no worries about being seen and had cavorted naked, swimming in the pool and lying in the sun. But they hadn't wanted to risk leaving Jason alone in the house. Instead they had brought him outside and tied him to a tree with belts from the wardrobe. After a while the leader of the pack, the part played by Camilla, had got bored and decided to give Jason her full attention, his cock already erect from watching the five naked women, two of whom had lain on the grass right in front of him, performing mutual cunnilingus.

Nancy dipped her hand into the pool of oil in her navel, bringing it up to Jason's cock just as Camilla's hand, on screen, smeared the sun-tan oil she had been using all over his erection. Nancy's hand squeezed hard, wanking up and down while her other finger burrowed between her legs plunging two, then three fingers into her sex and making herself moan and arch her body off the bed.

'You'll make me come,' Jason said.

'That's what I want. Come over my tits,' Nancy said

increasing the tempo of her hand just as she increased the tempo of her fingers stroking back and forth in her body.

She was not looking at him in person but staring at the screen. The women had bound him to the tree by pulling his arms behind him and around the trunk, binding his wrists with a leather strap. Not satisfied with this however, they had used more belts around his chest and waist and thighs and ankles to secure him tighter, forcing him back against the knarled, coarse bark of the tree and making it impossible for him to move an inch. Camilla was pressing her naked body against him, her arms wrapped around the tree so she could push herself against him harder, his cock sticking out between her tightly closed thighs, trapped and helpless.

'You look so turned on,' Nancy said almost to herself, her hand squeezing his cock as Camilla's sun-tan-oiled body squirmed against him on screen. She pulled her fingers out of her sex and went back to her clitoris, pushing it from side to side, then up and down, each movement producing a tremor of feeling.

On the screen the women had all gathered round to watch Camilla.

'Shall I make him come?' Camilla asked them.

'See how far it can reach,' Mandy said.

'Yeah, like this . . .' one of the others said, indicating that the girls should all lie in front of Jason side by side, like cars to be jumped by Evil Knievel.

Camilla moved around to the back of the tree, her arms wrapped round it, one hand on the shaft of his cock, the other holding his balls.

'You heard them, big boy. We want to see how far

you can spunk,' she hissed at him, her hand beginning to wank his cock again.

'Do it for me, baby,' Nancy whispered, not taking her eyes off the television, feelings running through her body like electricity.

He watched her fingers between her legs, her sex framed by the black suspender belt, the long fingers of the suspenders bisecting her thighs, as taut and tense as his cock. He could see her body quivering, her big breasts particularly, glistening with the oil she had spread on them. He knew he was coming. He glanced up at the screen showing a close-up of his cock being manipulated by Camilla's hands, one squeezing his balls rhythmically like some sort of exercise machine, while the other circled the rim of his glans and concentrated on stroking up and down over it. He was coming on screen too . . .

'Baby, spunk me, baby . . .' Nancy begged, just as Jason's screen cock lost control. Helplessly bound, unable to stop himself, his cock spasmed in Camilla's oily hands and spunk shot out in a wide arc, anointing each of the four girls who lay on the grass in front of him, spraying their breasts and bellies, each gob greeted with a squeal of delight as Camilla's hand pumped at his balls to extract every last drop.

Jason remembered how it had felt, how much the bark of the tree had cut his back, how much he had desperately wanted to be free, how he had ached to be able to throw himself on to one of the women, push his cock into them and fuck them, fuck what he knew would be their eager, hot wet sex. But he couldn't, he'd had to stand there and let his cock be wanked.

He looked down at Nancy, her finger working

incessantly at her clitoris. He'd every intention of doing what she asked, of letting her wank him, of spunking over her tits, until he'd remembered that feeling. It made something snap inside him. Without thinking he tore her hand away from his cock and literally leaped on to her body, almost knocking the breath out of her, his cock pushing her hand out of the way as it dived, in one seamless movement, between her legs and up into the depths of her cunt.

'Jesus . . .' she screamed, his cock so hard and hot it felt like red-hot steel drilling into her.

He hammered into her, his buttocks rising and falling like a hammer, ploughing his way up into her cunt, wanting to open her, wanting to do nothing but please himself, not caring about her pleasure, only caring about his own, the memory of the frustration on the film, so graphically portrayed, driving him on.

'Jason, Jason . . .' Nancy moaned, completely carried away by his passion, feeling his cock pounding deeper and deeper, drenched in her juices. She had been on the point of coming on her own hand, but now his cock was taking her higher, wiping out the previous high, making her want more, making her want to feel her orgasm break on the hardness and heat of his cock.

In a moment she would be over the edge, unable to do anything. Using all her self-control, she worked her hand down between their navels, up between her legs, up until she could feel Jason's shaft plunging into her, and her own labia spread open. Hooking her finger down, she pushed it into her body, right up into her sex alongside Jason's cock. It was the last thing she did. As she felt her cunt expand, as her own finger penetrated her sex, stretching it even further apart, she felt Jason's reaction to the new intruder.

'I'm coming...' he managed to gasp. He squirmed against her oily breasts, feeling her nipples as hard as stone, just as he could feel her finger working against his cock.

'Yes... yes...'

And they came together, exactly at the same moment. Nancy's orgasm making her sex contract, sucking his cock and her finger deeper at exactly the moment his cock started to spasm and the first jet of spunk lashed into her. She felt it pulse against her finger, felt his hot spunk, and that took her higher, just as the feeling of her sex convulsing on him, clinging to him so hot and wet, took him higher too, jerked his cock harder, made him spit out even more of his spunk.

For minutes they clung together panting for air. Slowly Nancy pulled her finger out. She licked it. It tasted of spunk.

'Umm...' she said enthusiastically. 'Tastes so good.'

'Where did you get that idea?'

'Just came to me. What about you? Anyone would think you hadn't had sex for a week.'

'It was that scene...'

'What, the one by the pool?'

'Why did you choose that one?'

'I like to see you spunk. I wanted you to spunk over my tits.'

'You're not complaining are you?'

'No. Anyway, Camilla's got beautiful hands.'

'And what? You were imagining them touching you?'

'We should invite her round again. Do you think she would come?'

'Come?' he said laughing.
'Come round,' Nancy hit his arm.
'I'm sure she would if I remember what happened last time.'
'I certainly do.'
'Call her.'
'Don't worry, I will.'

Chapter Three

'Hello?'

'Hello, stranger.'

'Who is that?'

'Don't you remember? I should be offended. I didn't think I was someone you'd easily forget.'

Jason tried to think who the voice on the phone might be. It certainly sounded familiar, soft tones of a New England American accent, but he could just not put a face to it.

'Sorry,' was all he could say.

'Well, I remember you. In fact I remember every detail...'

'I wish I could say the same.' It was true. The voice was alluring.

'Oh, I think you'll remember most of it, unless of course you make a habit of fucking the wives of the heads of film studios while their husbands look on...'

'Helen Talbot,' he said at once.

'Very good. Now do you remember?'

'How could I ever forget?'

'Exactly.'

'It's nice to hear from you.'

'Why didn't you call me? I asked you to.'

'Oh, I thought I was *persona non grata* as far as you were concerned.'

'Why should you think that?'

'It was what I was told. Hanna Silverstein spread a

lot of stories about me. About what I was supposed to have done.'

'True stories?'

'No.'

'I thought not.'

'You heard them?'

'Sure. Hanna called Bill. Bill told me. Hanna's a first-class bitch, Jason. Everyone knows that. Unfortunately she's a talented bitch so people put up with it. She's also very temperamental. You got on her wrong side is all.'

'So I've been told.'

'Does that mean you should forget your friends?'

'Are you my friend?'

'Sure I am. I thought we were going to get together. Don't you remember what I said? Then you disappear. I've been trying to get your number for ages. It would have been so much simpler if you'd called me.'

'I wasn't to know, was I? I thought you'd been warned off like everyone else.'

'No one warns me off, Jason. Have you got a pencil?'

Jason searched around the worktop of Nancy's kitchen where he had answered the phone. He found a pen hanging on a string from a cork noticeboard covered with recipes, messages and advertisements for home-delivery restaurants.

'Yes,' he said.

'One thousand three hundred and fifty Malibu Canyon Drive. Got that?'

'Yes, but . . .'

'Come along at two this afternoon.'

She didn't ask him if he could make it or say goodbye. The next thing Jason knew the dialling tone was sounding in his ear.

RETURN TO THE CASTING COUCH

Jason hung the handset back in the bright chromium hook of the receiver which was screwed to the kitchen wall. He was not at all sure he cared for the way he had been summoned to Helen Talbot's presence without being asked whether he would like to come around or not. Perhaps she assumed that that detail had been taken care of at their last meeting. There was, however, no doubt in his mind that he would go. Mrs Talbot's husband was the head of a major studio. Not only might renewing his friendship with her be productive in terms of Len Furey's film, it was also Talbot's studio that was putting up the money for *The Casting Couch*. He would take any chance he had to find out what was happening on that film, however peremptorily he had been summoned.

He knew, of course, that Mrs Helen Talbot had not invited him around for a cosy chat. The Talbots had a very unusual marriage in terms of their sex lives. Mr Talbot's sexual pleasure came from seeing Mrs Talbot being fucked and buggered by other men, mostly total strangers. That was his turn-on and Mrs Talbot, a beautiful willowy blonde, acquiesced willingly, apparently enjoying the experience as much as her husband and recompensed no doubt, if she did not, by living in a huge mansion in total luxury with charge accounts at every store on Rodeo Drive.

His first encounter with Helen Talbot had been at Hanna Silverstein's instigation and with her husband watching avidly. His second, however, had been more private and he remembered her suggesting that she would like to be alone with him again. Whether this was her intention now or whether her husband would be there to watch, he did not know. Either way this was definitely not an opportunity to be missed.

He smiled at himself broadly. He suddenly realised that his first thought had not been of a sexual liaison with an extremely beautiful woman, but of what the meeting might do for his career! Nancy was always telling him to 'be more Hollywood'. Well, he thought with a grin, he was obviously learning.

The taxi stopped in front of the barred private driveway, its wheels kicking up a cloud of the fine powdery sand from the dusty track. A private security guard emerged from a white-painted hut, a gun holstered on his belt, and peered into the back seat of the cab, a clipboard in his hand.

'Yeah?' he asked.

'Jason MacIver to see Mrs Talbot.'

'Mac what?'

'Iver. I.V.E.R.'

He consulted his clipboard. 'Oh. Right. Got you. Just go down to the beach and hang a left. It's the big house built outa the cliff.'

'Thanks.'

Slowly, with no urgency, the guard returned to his hut and operated the button that raised the barrier. The taxi-driver gunned the engine and, with another cloud of dust, headed down towards the sea.

They were in a steep-sided but not very deep canyon that soon opened out to a long white sandy beach. An amazing collection of houses of every sort lined the road, everything from small clapboard cottages to a vast mansion with Corinthian columns that would not have looked out of place in Virginia during the Civil War.

The unmade road, pitted with numerous holes, came to an end some two hundred yards in front of the beach. There was no need to ask directions to the Talbot house. It could be seen quite clearly, a replica of a Frank Lloyd Wright house, cantilevered out of solid rock, dominating the view. A long winding path, set with concrete steps, led up to it from the shore.

'Big house,' the black taxi-driver volunteered, the first words he'd spoken all trip.

'Looks impressive.'

'You an actor?' he asked as he searched for change in a suede money bag, Jason only having a twenty-dollar bill. 'They all live round here. That house there's Larry Hagman's. You know *Dallas*? You get *Dallas* in England?' He pronounced it Dall-ass.

'Sure,' Jason replied, correcting himself immediately to 'yes', when he realised he was using an Americanism. He wanted to be careful about his accent.

'Have a nice day,' the driver said as Jason tipped him two dollars and got out of the cab.

It was a beautiful day. Here on the coast, the LA smog was dispelled by the light breeze off the sea. The air, heavy with ozone, smelt clean, and small white clouds floated aimlessly across the clear blue sky. Jason walked down to the shoreline and along to the steps that led up to the spectacular beach house.

It was a steep climb but Jason kept himself in good shape and was hardly out of breath when he reached the top. Concrete steps led to a small paved patio, scattered with numerous flowering plants in terracotta pots and several lemon trees already bearing fruit. A small door was set in the exterior wall, a bell push to one side of it below a video security camera. He pushed the doorbell twice but could hear no corresponding sound. In no more than three or four seconds the door sprung open with a loud click.

Jason let himself into the house and closed the door behind him. He found himself in a narrow hallway, at the end of which he could see a tall window overlooking the sea. He walked down to a big rectangular room, the room that could be seen from outside projecting from the cliff. Its walls were glass from top to bottom on three sides. The cliff was a promontory that jutted out into the sea so the coastline to the north and south could be seen right down to the pier and Alice's Restaurant on one side, and a broken rocky shore on the other. People swam in the sea, joggers ran up and down, a few surfboards were being used with little success as the ocean was calm, but mostly the majority of the beach population, Jason could see, were lying lazily in the hot sun.

At the back of the room, above the hallway through which Jason had entered, was a gallery with a beautifully designed spiral staircase in one corner giving access to it. Each step of the spiral was inset with a complex pattern of marquetry reflecting the pattern of the staircase itself.

There was no sight nor sound of Helen Talbot.

Tentatively, Jason mounted the staircase. He looked down at the huge room. Everything in it was either antique – a Louis XV escritoire in burr elm, a George III mahogany four-pillar dining table with matching chairs – or ultra modern, furniture obviously especially commissioned from craftsmen whose work was particularly notable. As there was only one wall to hang paintings, on which was displayed a set of Baxt prints, most of the art in the room was modern sculpture. Jason recognised a Dali, a Henry Moore bronze and a Hepworth. The wooden floor, in ash, was scattered with handwoven wool rugs.

There were two doors off the gallery and a corridor. Trying both the doors he found them locked. He listened again for the sound of any activity, but could hear none. He started down the corridor, long and narrow and rather dark. He had convinced himself that he knew what to expect now. This was all part of the game. He would open one of the doors and find Helen Talbot, probably naked, lying on a large double bed, her husband sitting in an armchair drawn up besides her, watching her and waiting – waiting for her to be fucked – and he would be required to perform. He couldn't have been more wrong.

There were four doors in the corridor. He opened the first door behind which was a luxurious bedroom, though obviously not the master suite. The second and third were bedroom and bathroom respectively. There was only one door left, facing him at the far end of the passage. Clearly, he thought, without taxing his powers of deduction too thoroughly, Helen Talbot was waiting for him behind this door. He took a deep breath and got ready to give his performance.

Hesitantly he opened the door. Obviously this was the master bedroom. It was a vast room, a huge window overlooking the sea to the side of the house, a canopied double bed placed for the best view, and very little furniture besides. Outside the window was a small terrace with white tables and chairs and a single wooden lounger. One of the windows was open and a slight breeze ruffled the lace curtains that veiled the glass. But the room was deserted.

Puzzled, Jason looked around. There were two doors on the far wall. He opened the nearest to find a long rectangular dressing room, one of its longest walls lined with dress rails, the other with banks of drawers all labelled with the items they contained. Above the drawers were shelves for hats and luggage. On the short walls, racks were fitted to hold countless pairs of shoes, like the clothes, all for women. The other short wall was lined from floor to ceiling with a mirror. Again there was no sign of Helen Talbot.

Back in the bedroom Jason found the other door led to a marble bathroom – a black marble bathroom with white fittings – but that was deserted too and there was no other exit. The whole house appeared to be empty.

Of course, Jason knew someone had to be in, someone had operated the door lock. He stood and listened. For a moment he heard nothing but then thought he detected a slight noise. He listened intently. He heard the noise again, though he couldn't say what it was. He tried to work out where it was coming from. It seemed to be in the direction of the dressing room. He opened the dressing room door again. The noise was definitely louder when it came this time, but where could it possibly be coming from?

Feeling rather silly, he parted the clothes on the rails to see if there was a hidden door behind them. There wasn't. He noticed the door he had come in through had closed of its own accord. He hadn't noticed that behind the shoe racks the wall and the back of the door was mirrored, just like the wall at the other end of the room. With the door closed, so perfectly was it fitted, it was difficult to imagine there was a door there at all. It had no handle or lock. He pushed on the glass and it swung out again, then closed quietly, obviously on some sort of strong gravity hinge.

Walking down the length of the room, he went to examine the mirror at the other end, working on the principle that if one concealed a door so successfully so might the other. Sure enough, as soon as he got close, he saw a thin line where the glass had been cut. He pushed the glass on the same spot he had pushed the other door and it opened.

At exactly that moment the bright fluorescent lights went out in the dressing room.

Apprehensively, Jason walked through the mirrored door. The room beyond was windowless and dark, its walls, ceiling and floor all black. The only light came from a single overhead spotlight, its beam illuminating a tight circle of light below. In the centre of the circle Jason stared at a most extraordinary sight. Helen Talbot was lying on her back on what resembled a vaulting horse with tapering legs, its rectangular surface just wide enough and long enough to support her torso and head. Like a vaulting horse the top was padded and covered in thick suede. Most of Helen's bottom was hanging over its edge. Her legs were raised in the air, her ankles strapped into leather cuffs through the D-rings of which white ropes had been passed. The ropes were attached to a pulley on two wooden pillars on either side of the base, about six feet apart, and tied off so that Helen's legs were spread wide apart and lifted at about a twenty degree angle above the plane of her body. Her arms were bound too, her wrists held together in leather cuffs like the ones on her ankles, then pulled back over her head and tied to a crosspiece that ran between the legs at the bottom of the frame, securing her hands under the back of her head, her elbows sticking out like chicken wings. The only movement her bondage would allow was in her elbows. She could bring them together in front of her face, or spread them apart on either side of her body. Neither movement made much difference to her captivity.

A small black leather ball had been inserted in her mouth and was secured in place by a black leather strap. The ball distended her cheeks slightly.

Helen Talbot's beautiful and bound body was naked – Jason had been right about that at least. Kneeling between her open legs was a woman he had never seen before. She had short red hair and was wearing a black leather leotard, long, elbow-length leather gloves and high-heeled leather boots. He could not see her face properly as it was buried in Helen's sex. He could see her tongue licking her labia, sparsely covered as they were by wispy blonde pubic hair, licking it like a child licks an ice cream, exaggeratedly long strokes taking in the whole furrow of her sex.

Jason's first reaction was to look around for a camera, or a mirror that could be used to hide a camera, or an audience. He had been caught before, his sexual adventures shot on film without his knowledge, and he had no intention of letting it happen again, even for private viewing. As far as he could see, though, there was nowhere a camera could be concealed and there was certainly no mirrors.

'You're late,' the redhead said, getting to her feet and wiping her mouth.

'I couldn't find it,' Jason said. 'No one gave me directions.'

'Helen told me you'd been here before.'

'No. That was the other house...'

'Well, get your clothes off then,' she said casually, as if she was asking him to change a light bulb. 'I'm Honey.' She did not offer to shake his hand or kiss his cheek.

Jason wondered if Bill Talbot was watching. As he unbuttoned his shirt, he looked around the room again trying to peer into the dark corners. Honey read his mind.

'He's not here,' she said. 'He never comes here.'

Jason wanted to ask why but decided not to. He pulled his shoes and socks off then threw aside his shirt, watching Honey who stood gently caressing Helen's exposed inner thigh. She was short and the leather leotard was tight on her slightly overweight figure, cut high on the hips to reveal her long plump flanks, its crotch so tight the leather had folded itself into the crease of her sex. Her breasts, as far as he could judge, were small as there was little cleavage at the V-neck of the garment. Her face too was chubby, a little too solid and unrefined to be beautiful, her deep green eyes dull and unexcited as though they had seen too much of the world.

'Come on, you're not shy are you? You didn't look shy on screen...' she mocked. Obviously Helen Talbot had also been privy to an early copy of *Escape of the Whores*.

Jason skimmed his jeans and boxer shorts off his legs. At the moment, despite Helen's nakedness and bondage, he did not feel in the least turned on. He had been expecting one thing and was rapidly having to readjust to another. He had definitely not been expecting anything so bizarre.

'You not into this scene?' Honey asked, looking at his flaccid cock.

'I don't know...'

'Oh come on, beautiful doll like this all trussed up like Thanksgiving Turkey. She loves it. Loves being abused... Silly bitch.'

Jason could believe that. He had had one of the strangest experiences of his life the first time he had met Helen Talbot. He was quite prepared to believe what he had been asked to do that night was only the tip of the iceberg as far as she was concerned.

'You're a slut, aren't you?' Honey was saying, reinforcing the sentiment by slapping the thigh she had been caressing with her gloved hand. 'Aren't you?' she repeated when Helen did not attempt to reply.

Helen nodded vigorously and made a muffled sound that was meant to be a 'yes' through the gag.

Jason's head filled with questions. Who was Honey and where did she fit into the Talbot's *ménage*? Was she paid for whatever services she delivered and how often did Helen indulge herself in this black room? More importantly, what was he supposed to do?

The last question he asked. 'What do you want me to do?'

'I've never understood men. You're faced with this and you don't know what to do.'

'This is what she wants?'

'Look at her. She's so hot for it she's melting.' Honey was looking at Helen's sex. The position of her legs had spread it wide open, the sparse hair concealing nothing. Jason could see the mouth of her vagina and below it the puckered core of her anus. All of it was shining in the strong spotlight, her wetness leaking copiously from her body running down to the edge of the base where it had stained the suede.

Honey moved around the wooden pillar that supported one of Helen's legs to stand by her side. Helen's breasts were big and pendulous. They had flopped over to the side of her chest and were hanging down her sides. Honey picked one up in both gloved hands and started to knead it. With her other hand she used one finger to stroke the outline of Helen's face, tracing around her eyes and nose and both lips separated by the ball gag.

Tentatively, Jason positioned himself between Helen's bound legs. In his time in Hollywood he had been in some very strange situations and been asked to perform some very strange acts. It hadn't fazed him. If he were honest with himself he had enjoyed it, even though none of the fantasies he had helped to fulfil were of his own making. He had taken it in his stride. Now he knew he had to perform again. Not only was Helen Talbot's husband a very important person, but so far Helen had been the only one who had not taken Hanna Silverstein's stories at face value. He didn't want to lose that.

'What shall we do with the bitch then?' he said, testing his intonation as he might test the lines for a new part.

'She loves this,' Honey said, slapping her gloved hand down on Helen's breast.

'Does she?' Jason raised his hand and smacked it down on Helen's thigh. She moaned. 'Oh, you do . . .'

He slapped her six times, three times on each thigh, hard stinging blows that reddened Helen's white skin. Each stroke produced a muffled moan, but it was clear that the underlying note was pleasure.

Helen lifted her head. She was looking at Jason for the first time since he'd come into the black room. Her marine-blue eyes were sparkling with excitement. He saw them flick down from his face, down his naked body to her own sex, spread open and framed by her thighs. What she saw – her helplessness, the bounds that held her ankles, her two tormentors clearly increased her pleasure, like a transformer stepping up the voltage of an electric current. Her body shuddered before she rested her head back down again.

Jason used both hands to caress her inner thighs where his slaps had turned them pale pink. They were radiating heat. He moved his fingers until they were nudging against her labia. It was so easy to work on her in this position, her sex at waist height laid out in front of him. It looked like something apart from her, with its own life, pulsing and alive, its gorge clearly visible, a dark crimson. He probed it with his finger as though it were a strange botanical specimen he had never seen before. With his other hand, he exposed the little pink bud of her clitoris, hiding under the fleshy petals of her labia. He heard another muffled moan, two distinct tones for each intrusion. Her clitoris, like the rest of her sex, was swollen and engorged, the nectar of her body making everything glisten.

Honey ducked down, crawled under Helen's suspended leg and knelt at Jason's side. Taking his buttocks in her hands, she twisted him around slightly so she could hoover up his cock into her mouth. Now, it was his turn to moan. Honey's mouth felt like silk, moulding itself to the contours of his cock, sucking it in like a baby on a teat, sucking him to full erection in seconds.

Jason tried to concentrate on Helen, pushing two fingers into her cunt, then three. Then, remembering how he had been made to use her before, used the juices that had run down into the crater of her anus to lubricate his thumb and plunge that too inside her, into the tight tube of her arse. He watched his hand working, one moving back and forth inside her body, the other drawing imaginary circles on the tiny nodule of her clit.

Helen's head came up again, looking down her body to see what he was doing to her. But she could not hold it up for long and, as waves of pleasure broke over her, she lowered it again, her elbows coming together in front of her face, her body raked with feeling.

'I'm coming,' she screamed, though the words were not recognisable.

Jason didn't need to be told. As Honey sucked his cock, her fingers jiggling his balls, he drove his fingers into the two openings of her body one last time, knowing the moment was right. He drove them as high as they would go, till the tendons of his hand ached with the strain, up and up and up, while his other hand pressed down on her clitoris. He felt her body convulse, her cunt and anus contract together around his invading hand, a rush of juices flooding over him as though she had spunked. He watched it all, almost clinically. Her body went rigid, every nerve and muscle stretched against the bonds that held her, arching off the horse, then suddenly going limp, falling back, her energy gone, not a single part of her untouched by the aftermath of completion.

Honey pulled his cock from her mouth. 'Now fuck her, big boy . . .' she said, pushing his cock round towards Helen's sex.

'No!' Jason said decisively. Perhaps it was the way Honey assumed he was there to be told what to do, or perhaps it was just the whole situation, but dramatically Jason's mood changed. He was being used again. Despite Helen's helplessness she was the one who was calling the shots, not him. He felt a wave of anger, caught Honey's hand and tugged it off his cock.

'She likes it . . .' Honey said, not understanding.

'But I don't. Get her down.'

Honey looked puzzled. Helen raised her head and shook it from side to side.

'Do it,' he ordered with absolute determination, pulling Honey to her feet.

Honey looked from Jason to Helen then back to Jason. The look in his eyes convinced her she should do what he said and she quickly untied the ropes on the pulleys that held Helen's legs in the air. She went round to the top of the horse and knelt to release the bindings that held the leather cuffs at her wrists. Helen sat up. The gag still distorted her face but her annoyance was clear.

Jason took no notice. A few minutes ago he was concerned about what she wanted. Now he simply didn't care. His own lust had taken over. The white rope that had bound her wrists to the bottom of the horse was still attached to the central link that held the two cuffs together. Jason grabbed it and pulled Helen off the bench. Without looking at her, the rope in his hand like a leash on a dog, he stormed out of the black room, through the dressing room and out into the daylight of the bedroom, jerking so fiercely on the rope to make Helen follow that she almost tripped over.

In the bedroom, he threw her on her back on the bed and fell on top of her, not caring about anything but his need, his need to have her, to bury his cock inside her. Her sex, not surprisingly considering what he had been doing to it, was liquid and molten and Jason's cock was as hard as a bone. He buried it inside her, as deep as it would go and then tried to force it deeper, arching his whole body to push his cock forward.

'Oh . . .' she moaned through the gag. She raised her legs on either side of him, her ankles still strapped in rings of leather, until they were at right angles to her body, increasing his penetration still further, her arms stretched out above her head.

Honey had followed them through into the bedroom. She sat at the foot of the bed watching.

'Quite a show . . .' she said.

'Take the gag out,' Jason ordered, looking over his shoulder at the redhead.

Honey did as she was told, unstrapping the ball gag from Helen's mouth. Before she could say a word, Jason replaced it with his mouth, plunging his tongue between her lips, her mouth as hot and wet as her sex. She sucked on it, then tried to push it aside to get her tongue into him.

He felt her big meaty breasts trapped under his chest, their nipples like stone. He felt her sex clasping him like a fist, her copious juices running down his balls. Slowly he pulled his cock out of her, until he could feel her labia again, then rammed it back up suddenly, taking her breath away. In and out, out slowly, then slamming back in, each inward stroke making her gasp.

His mouth left her lips. He kissed her long neck. His hand found her nipple. She was a beautiful woman. He looked down at her and watched her react, her body visibly thrilling, as he slammed his cock into her.

'Don't stop . . .' she begged.

'I thought you didn't want this . . .' he taunted.

'I do, I do . . . please . . .'

He was driving into her faster and faster, his own need impossible to control, spunk pumping into his shaft, his cock throbbing.

'Oh yes, yes, yes . . .' she was mouthing continuously, each word provoked by the upward thrust of his cock.

Honey positioned herself at the foot of the bed. With Helen's legs raised so high, she could see everything – the whole length of Jason's cock sawing to and fro, Helen's labia stretched apart by its size, even the little bud of her anus glistening and wet. Slowly and deliberately, she reached forward and placed her leather-stalled forefinger on the little opening, rubbing the wetness into the puckered flesh. Then, as forcefully as Jason had rammed in his cock, Honey penetrated the rear passage, stuffing her finger right up as far as her knuckle would allow.

'God . . .' Helen howled.

Immediately, Jason felt Honey's finger pressing into the underside of his cock, through the thin membranes of Helen's body, making her cunt even tighter. He knew he wouldn't be able to resist this further provocation after so much else, but he didn't have to.

RETURN TO THE CASTING COUCH

The new intrusion had the same effect on Helen. She was tossing her head from side to side on the bed, her hands, still bound, looping over Jason's back holding him tightly, her naked body trembling. Honey did not push her finger in and out; instead she turned it as far as it would go in one direction and then back and round in the other.

Helen felt her nerves begin to tingle, the waves of orgasm gathering. But it was Jason that made her come. With one final effort he arched his cock up into her, pushing it up, using every muscle to drive it deeper, as deep as it would go. She felt the cavern of her sex open out, as though he had burrowed through a secret cave, a new area of sensitivity exposed, new nerves, never touched before, prodded by his hot poker of a cock, the feeling making her explode, her orgasm raking through every sense, a scream of pleasure forced from her wide-open mouth.

Jason did not withdraw again. There was no need. He felt Honey's finger moving against his cock, inside Helen's body, and then her other hand closing on his balls, gathering them in until she had them both in her palm. Gently but firmly she squeezed them, at the same time pulling them away from his cock. Instantly, as if she had thrown a switch, his cock spasmed, kicking against the tight confines of Helen's inner sex, and great strings of spunk jetted out into her, against the silky wet walls, Honey's hand kneading his balls as if milking them.

Helen reacted too. Jason's cock had swollen as he spunked, pushing deeper into her, stretching the tight tunnel that surrounded it, filling her even more, making her feel again the energy and power that had made her come in the first place, and this provoked another orgasm, sudden and savage, tearing through her nerves, her body taken by surprise with its ferocity.

Gradually Jason's senses returned. He felt Honey unstrapping the cuffs that bound Helen's hands. He looked down into Helen's eyes, but she had not recovered as quickly, her eyes still glazed and unfocused.

As Jason rolled off her, Honey immediately knelt between Helen's thighs, stripping off her long leather gloves and caressing the soft creamy flesh with the fingertips of both hands.

'Mmm...' Helen said approvingly.

'You haven't finished yet have you,' Honey said. It was not a question, but as if by way of an answer Helen turned towards Jason, who was lying by her side.

'Up here,' she said. 'I want to taste it.'

There was no doubt what she meant. Jason squirmed up the bed and, the second he was in reach, she clamped her mouth over his flaccid cock, tasting her own juices.

Jason could not stop himself from moaning. Helen's mouth was hot, very hot. He could hear her sucking on the liquid coating and swallowing what she gleaned. Her tongue licked at the rim of his glans, oversensitised by his orgasm, and made him shudder. But he did not stop her. Releasing his cock for a moment she licked at his balls, holding his shaft out of the way with her fingers, her tongue lapping up the rich slick of sap that clung to the hairs of his scrotum.

'Taste good, don't you, baby?' Honey said.

'Mmm,' Helen muttered, knowing that Honey meant to taste for herself, spreading her legs further apart, and angling her sex up towards the redhead.

RETURN TO THE CASTING COUCH

Honey dipped her head into Helen's crotch, the sparse pubic hair of her labia plastered down by its wetness.

'God...' Helen cried as Honey's lips touched her labia, kissing it as though it were a mouth, squirming against it and darting her tongue in and out of its centre, tasting Helen's juices and Jason's spunk.

Jason watched Honey's red hair bobbing between Helen's legs. As she moved her mouth against Helen's sex, he saw that her right hand had groped over her own back, down between her legs, and was working to free the clasps that held the crotch-piece of the leather leotard in place. He heard a definite click as they were torn free.

Helen's mouth was more demanding now, sucking his cock harder, her tongue skating over the surface of his glans looking for the most sensitive places. He felt himself starting to grow, the heat of Helen's mouth, and the evidence of his eyes, making him recover his lust. Both Honey's hands were snaking up above her head, along Helen's body, to find her nipples. He saw her locate them, one after another, her fingers pinching and pulling on them, the effect this had further increasing the heat of Helen's mouth on his swelling cock.

'Fuck her...' Helen said, her mouth leaving Jason the moment she felt him fully erect.

'Mmm...' Honey said, wriggling her arse from side to side by way of welcoming the idea.

'She needs cock too...'

Jason looked down at his erection. It was red and wet with Helen's saliva. It felt incredibly hard again, the stimulus of these two women too much to ignore.

He got to his feet as Helen lay back on the bed, her legs spread, her big breasts in Honey's hands, her eyes bright with excitement, her mouth slack and her lips wet from the juices she'd sucked from Jason's cock. He looked at Honey, her head tucked between Helen's thighs, her knees under her chest in a neat little ball, the crotch-piece of the black leather leotard hanging loose at the base of her arse like a tail.

Kneeling behind her, Jason hooked his arms around Honey's thighs and pulled them apart, the fingers of one hand probing into the furrow of her sex. He found what he was looking for. Her clitoris was big, a swollen throbbing nut of flesh that had pushed its own way out from between her labia.

'Yes,' she said, the word muffled on Helen's sex.

She thrust her buttocks up into the air until she could feel Jason's cock, hot and hard between them, as he flicked the leather crotch-piece out of the way. Helen raised her head from the bed to see what was happening, just as she had when she'd been tied to the suede padded 'horse'.

With his finger still on her inflated clit, Jason bucked his hips back, nosed his cock down between Honey's thighs and felt the mouth of her sex parting to admit him.

'Fuck her, Jason,' Helen said in a very steady cool voice.

He needed no second bidding, the sight of the two women more than enough provocation. He bucked his hips again and slid into Honey's cunt, but only an inch or so. Her passage was tight, so tight in fact he thought he had made a mistake and was ploughing her anus. He moved his finger back to reassure himself, and felt his cock surrounded by Honey's moist labia. He pushed again. Her vagina was wet but very, very tight.

He saw Helen watching, supporting her head by resting both hands behind it, wanting to see everything. He heard Honey moan as he lunged forward again. He had never felt anything so tight. He couldn't get all the way in. She was just too small. He plunged on, each time opening her more, getting deeper.

Helen felt her body pulse. Jason's fine muscular body and Honey's mouth were producing waves of pleasure in her, each of Jason's efforts to get deeper into Honey's sex provoking an exclamation of pleasure that drove hot breath against Helen's clitoris.

Jason had got as far in as he was going to get. He had never felt anything like Honey's cunt. It seemed to grip him, squeeze him, holding him so tightly it allowed him to move very little. Then he felt an entirely new sensation. Honey's cunt began to contract rhythmically, like a powerful muscle, squeezing his cock, milking it, as strong as any hand, except this hand was hot and wet and fitted itself perfectly to every contour of his shaft.

'Great . . .' he moaned.

Honey loved this, loved having a cock trapped inside her. It turned her on, and she knew no man could resist. She had practised for hours on dildoes, perfected her technique, the muscles of her sex as powerful as any in her body. Their movement moved her clitoris in turn, building her own climax at the same time she milked Jason of his.

Her excitement, the waves of pleasure pulsing through her body, communicated itself to Helen by the perfect medium of her mouth. Just as surely as her cunt was bringing Jason off again, so her mouth, her hot breath, her artful tongue, her pinching fingers, were having the same effect on Helen, her body already swimming with the aftermath of orgasm.

'Honey, Honey . . .' Helen gasped, as the tongue that had licked her so many times before circled her clitoris in the most perfect pattern, each circuit making her body tremble with a whole gamut of emotion. She managed to keep her eyes open long enough to see the expression on Jason's face – the lust, the need. She could see his body pressed into Honey's plump, full arse, and Honey's head framed by her own open thighs, and that image, burnt into her mind, like the bright sun on the retina, took her over the edge and hurtling down, once again, to a shattering completion.

Honey felt it as if it were her own, felt it on Helen's labia and clitoris, felt a gush of juices almost at the same moment she felt Jason's cock throbbing inside her, the big muscle of her sex relentless, squeezing him rhythmically, tightly, hotly, until more spunk pumped up into his cock.

Jason looked at the two women: Helen's body now slack and replete; Honey's, on the other hand, tense and rigid, her back covered in black leather, her thighs parted for him. He was being milked, milked of his spunk and he loved it. He could no longer keep his eyes open. But that did not mean his mind was not full of images – images of Helen, tied and spread in the black room, of his fingers inside her, of Honey sucking his cock . .

'Oh God . . .' he gasped, as the spunk he had no idea he had shot from his body, and absolute sensation made him convulse, his cock trying to jerk against its imprisonment, but not succeeding, this feeling too, somehow adding to his pleasure.

Then it was Honey's turn. Relaxing completely, her body awash with spunk, she thrust her buttocks back at Jason.

'Fuck me...' she ordered.

He knew what she needed. Before his erection started to dwindle, he plunged into her wildly, wanting to give her what she had given him. He felt her sex relax, allowing him in, deeper and deeper at every stroke, as though her body was melting over him. He held her by the hips her fingers digging into her flesh, as he rode his cock up into her.

'That's it!' she screamed. 'Oh yes, that's it.'

He was right up her now, his balls, for the first time, banging against her labia. He reamed into her, feeling his own hot spunk at the top of her sex.

'That's it... that's...' She couldn't finish the sentence. Her body went rigid and she felt as though she was falling, falling into a pit of ecstasy, every nerve in her body swamped with pleasure, wallowing in it, the head of Jason's cock thrust so deeply inside her it felt as though it would split her in two.

'That's it,' she said quietly when she was able to say anything at all.

It was a big hot tub on the terrace overlooking the sea, though not overlooked itself, the wooden structure built like an enormous barrel, set into teak decking that covered the whole area. The tub was fitted with a powerful jacuzzi that could be turned on from a switch by the edge, and there were seats in the water to allow the occupants to sit and lean against the wooden sides.

'You haven't been introduced properly,' Helen said in her cultured New England accent. She was already sitting naked in the hot water. 'This is Honey... my honey,' she added smiling.

Honey was pulling off a towelling robe while Jason brought a tray of glasses and a bottle of red wine, putting it on the decking within reach of the tub.

'I think it's a bit late for formalities,' he said, kneeling to pour the wine.

Honey stepped into the tub and waded over to Helen, who embraced her and kissed her affectionately on the cheek before she sat down beside her. Jason stripped off the towel he was wearing round his waist, distributed the wineglasses and climbed into the water. It was a perfect temperature.

'Do you do this often?' he asked, not at all sure whether he meant taking a hot tub or the activities in the black room.

'Oh yes, don't we, Honey?'

'We like to have fun.'

'I thought you'd enjoy it too,' Helen said, continuing the ambiguity.

Jason sat next to Helen, the water coming up to his neck. It was very clear and he could see her big breasts floating like life buoys.

'I did.'

'Oh, so did I, Jason. You're so...' she searched for the right word '... passionate. I didn't think I wanted to be free but you certainly know what you want, don't you? And so strong...'

'He's great,' Honey said quietly. 'Great body.'

'You should see him on screen.'

'I did, remember?'

'We'll watch it again later... that scene where...'

'Can we talk about something else?' Jason asked. They were talking about him as if he wasn't there.

'Don't be so sensitive. You're fantastic in it, Jason.'

'I didn't come to LA to star in porn movies...'

'I know, I know, but it's better than nothing.' Helen's arm was round Honey's shoulders. Jason saw Honey's hand brushing Helen's floating breasts underwater.

'Do you know what's happening to *The Casting Couch*?'

'No. It's been postponed, that's all I know.'

'Hanna hasn't cast the lead yet?'

'Jason, I don't know, baby. If I knew I'd tell you, believe me.' Helen looked sympathetic.

'She's a bitch,' Honey said.

'Who?'

'Hanna. She's a real bitch.'

'Do you know her?' Helen asked.

'I knew a coupla guys she had. She used to come cruising down Venice beach looking for meat. She was hard. You were mixed up with her?' She looked at Jason with real admiration.

'So what are you going to do next?' Helen asked, her hand stroking Jason's arm.

'Len Furey's got this excellent script,' he said, delighted she'd brought the subject up. 'A thriller. He wants me to play the lead. It's got to be an Englishman. It was all set, then he lost the finance...'

'Same old story.'

'If he got that off the ground I'd be laughing.'

'Sounds good.'

'It's a great script. And an even better part for me.' He paused, wondering if he should go on. He decided to try, after all wasn't that the reason he'd agreed to come round? 'You don't think your husband would look at it, do you?'

'Bill? No. He wouldn't touch anything Len did. There's some sort of feud. Goes back a long way. These things always do.'

'Oh.' Jason looked crestfallen. He'd hoped Helen would say she'd persuade her husband to look at the script but if he didn't get on with Furey there would be no point. 'I thought he might be here . . .' he blurted out, trying to think of something to cover his disappointment.

'Bill never comes here. This is my house, everything in it belongs to me. My insurance in case some new blonde comes along with an even more compliant attitude.'

'Very sensible.'

'I give him what he wants at home but here is private. That's our understanding. Honey's private too.'

'I just thought that maybe . . .'

'Sure. We used you last time. But I told you, Jason, I wanted something more with you, more intimate. You turned me on. Most of the men my husband gets don't, period.'

Jason was thoroughly depressed. The afternoon had been a waste of time. Not only did he not have a chance of meeting Bill Talbot again, even in these bizarre circumstances, but there was no point in giving Helen a script for her husband to read. He smiled at himself, broadly realising the implications of this thought. He was definitely going native. He had just fucked two beautiful women, was drinking wine with them naked in a hot tub overlooking one of the most spectacular views he'd ever seen, and he was feeling depressed about his career!

'What's funny?' Helen asked sipping her wine. Honey's hand was on her navel stroking it underwater.

'Nothing.'

'So you need to get Len's film financed?'

'Yes.'

'Well, you met Harriet Teitelbaum didn't you, at Hanna's party?'

He had done more than just meet her. 'You could say that.' Though the water was hot and Jason's face already red, he was sure that he blushed at the mention of Harriet's name. 'I thought you'd left by then.'

'Hollywood's a small town, Jason.'

'It was another of Hanna's arrangements.'

'I bet it was. She'd do anything to keep in with Harriet. Any Hollywood producer would lick any part of her anatomy she cared to mention. She's the name of the game in this town. Did you get on with her?'

'I don't know.' The name had brought memories flooding back. Hanna Silverstein had a habit of 'lending' Jason to her friends, but with Harriet she had gone further, she had drugged him and allowed him to be used in a private sex show as the main exhibit.

'All right, put it another way, did you give her what she wanted?'

'Yes, I think so.'

'She had him fucking Cyn,' Honey added.

'You know Cynthia?' Jason said, looking surprised. Cynthia was Harriet's live-in girlfriend.

'Sure. We used to hang around gay clubs together. We got friendly 'cause we both liked the occasional man. Harriet took her off the street. Literally. She was working gay tricks off Hollywood and Vine . . . Been together ever since.'

'Did you?' Helen asked.

'What?'

'Fuck Cyn?'

'And the rest. It was quite a party.'

'So you see. You've got an in. Go and see her. Ask her to help.'

'You think she will?'

'No idea. It's worth a try, isn't it? I mean, you haven't got that many options . . .'

'True.'

'Well, then.' Honey's hand had slipped down between Helen's thighs and was burrowing into her pubic hair.

'You're so naughty,' Helen said, turning to kiss her full on the mouth. At the same time her other hand was fishing in the water for other game. Jason felt her fingers close on his cock.

'Put the jacuzzi on,' Helen said breathlessly, before returning to Honey's lips.

Jason pressed the rubber switch. A mass of bubbles and foam sprang up and underwater nozzles directed powerful jets as their bodies, pummelling their bodies. Jason felt his cock beginning to stir in Helen's hand.

'Looks like I've caught a nice big fish. I can feel it wriggling . . .' Helen said.

'Don't let it get away,' Honey said.

The two women got up and moved to the centre of the tub, Helen pulling Jason up by his cock. They stood in the foaming water, pressing their bodies into him,

Helen in front and Honey behind, making him the meat in their sandwich.

'And I thought we'd tired him out,' Helen said, feeling Jason's cock between her legs.

'Must be the company I keep,' Jason said as he felt her soft thighs closing around him and her big breasts, moved by the water, rubbing against his chest. He could feel Honey too, pushing herself into his back, her hard nipples against his shoulderblades . . .

Chapter Four

The office block was at the highest point on Sunset Boulevard, no more than ten stories, guaranteed earthquake-proof up to force nine on the Richter Scale. Its black windows reflected the sun, allowing not the slightest glimpse of what went on inside.

Jason took the lift to the top floor where Harriet's company, Teitelbaum Entertainment Holdings Incorporated, had its office.

A bright-faced blonde sat at a huge walnut desk immediately facing the lift doors. There was nothing on the desk but a tiny state-of-the-art switchboard and an enormous and very phallic stone sculpture that might have been Mexican. The reception area was as empty as the desk – a rich wool carpet, some modern tapestry on the walls and two leather armchairs that looked so uncomfortable they were clearly intended to put anyone off waiting. In front of them was a glass coffee table with copies of *Variety*, *Hollywood Reporter* and *Celebrity Bulletin* neatly arranged in line.

'May I help you?' the blonde said politely in what had hints of being a Texan drawl.

'I'd like to see Harriet Teitelbaum, please,' Jason said.

'Do you have an appointment?'

'No.'

'Well, you see nobody sees Ms –' she emphasised the 'Ms' heavily – 'Teitelbaum without an appointment.'

She sounded as if she was speaking to a young child.

'Could you just ask her secretary to tell her it's Jason MacIver?'

'Mac . . .'

'Iver. I.V.E.R.'

'I'll certainly do that for you, sir,' she said. 'Would you care to take a seat.' Her eyes were looking at Jason with interest, the way most women had looked at him since he was eighteen.

'Thank you.'

He manoeuvred himself into one of the cube-shaped leather chairs and watched as the blonde punched numbers into the keyboard on the console on the desk. The desk did not have a modesty panel and he could see her long slim legs underneath its surface. She crossed them, swivelling slightly from side to side on her office chair. He saw her mouth move but could not hear what she was saying. She put the phone down again.

He picked up the *Hollywood Reporter* from the table in front of him. He read through it without taking in a word, then started at the beginning again. He was halfway through it the second time when the blonde teetered up to him on spiky yellow high heels that matched her short yellow jersey dress.

'Sorry, Ms Teitelbaum will only see you if you have an appointment,' she said.

He was forced to look up her long legs. 'And how do I get an appointment?'

'Best is to write in.'

'Can't I just wait?'

'No. Really. She has her own private entrance. And I'd have to get security to throw you out. No one's allowed to wait.' She sounded genuinely apologetic.

'OK. I can take a hint.' With one final look at her glorious legs, he got up. 'I don't suppose you could give me her private address?'

'More than my job's worth.'

'I thought that's what you'd say. Thanks for your help anyway. You're very sweet.'

'See that,' the blonde said quietly as though someone might overhear. One wall of the reception area was thick plate glass, the whole wall with no frame. It was black on the outside but perfectly transparent from within. Immediately across the street was a bar, a red and blue neon sign forming the words, THE LUCKY STRIKE.

'The bar?' Jason said, following her gaze.

'Yeah. I finish at five,' she said.

Without another word she returned to her desk and answered an incoming call, leaving Jason to take the lift to the ground floor.

The Lucky Strike was a pastiche of a Western saloon, decorated with cow horns, fake colt revolvers, wagon wheels and other *objets d'art* from the period fabricated in a plaster shop that used to be part of a film studio. Jason ordered a diet cola from the cowgirl who served tables and looked at his watch. It was four o'clock. Exactly one hour later the blonde in the yellow dress walked in through the slatted swing doors and plumped her extremely shapely bottom on to the bentwood chair next to his.

'Hi,' she said. 'I take it you're going to buy me a drink?'

'I'd love to.'

'Bourbon rocks,' she said to the cowgirl who had

arrived at the table. 'Love your accent. Makes me shiver. I'm Cheryl.'

'Hello, Cheryl.'

'And you're Jason.'

'You remembered.'

'I certainly did.'

'So what can I do for you, Cheryl?'

'I thought it was more what I could do for you.'

'Like what?'

'Harriet Teitelbaum's address.'

'Really?'

'Let's put it this way – if by chance, this afternoon I happened to have written her private address on a little slip of paper while no one was looking, that would be worth something, wouldn't it?'

'Like what?'

'Like you.'

'Me?'

'Oh come on, don't be coy. You know the effect you have on women. I'm not the first to have spent the last hour leaking into her panties thinking about you.'

'You want me?'

The cowgirl delivered the bourbon to the table and set it down on a little white paper coaster in front of Cheryl, who picked it up and took a large swig immediately.

'Do you think that would be a fair exchange?'

'Very fair.'

'Good.' She reached into a small yellow handbag that perfectly matched the colour of her high heels and extracted a folded piece of paper. She held it up between two fingers, her fingernails carefully manicured and varnished. 'Deal?' she said.

'Deal.'

'Say it then. I want to hear it in that accent of yours...'

'Say what?'

'Something along the lines of what you'd like to do to me. How you'd like to take me and screw me...'

'Cheryl, I'd love to take you, strip off all your clothes and lick that beautiful body of yours all over...'

'Mmm... that's good.'

Jason looked at the piece of paper still held in her fingers.

'But what I'd really like to do, Cheryl,' he continued, 'is to bend you over, pull down those damp little panties and fuck the arse off you...'

'Mmm... really good,' She squirmed in her seat. 'I think I could come in my panties just listening to you.'

'I really want to fuck you, Cheryl.' And now it was true. He would have done it to get the address, of course, but looking across the table at her – the skirt of the dress hiding no more than the top inch of her slender, contoured thighs, the heavy swell of her bosom under the yellow jersey, and the way her rich full lips were slightly open and slightly wet – he would have done it for nothing. There was something in her face, a need, an excitement he wanted to test.

'Sounds so much better when you say it.'

'I mean it.'

'Do you live far from here?'

'No, that's not what I had in mind...'

'What then?'

'I've got a thing about cars...'

'I haven't got a car.'

'But I have. And it's got a great back seat.' She

finished her drink and handed him the slip of paper. 'And it's parked right across the street. Shall we go . . . ?'

His memory was hazy, to say the least. He remembered they had put him in the back of a big stretch Cadillac after Hanna had drugged his drink. The effect of the drug hadn't been very dramatic. It had just made the edges of reality blur and had done funny things to the passage of time, so one moment he appeared to be just getting into the car and the next it had driven miles. It had made him compliant, easier to handle and less aware of what was going on all around him.

He did remember being driven into a tunnel and the tunnel turning into an underground car park. But now, standing in front of the apartment block – a six-storey building in an ultra-modern design – where Cheryl had told him Harriet Teitelbaum had the penthouse, the only thing he could remember at all was the tunnel, which in fact turned out to be a ramp leading down to the basement, its entrance beautifully constructed in an elaborate herringbone pattern of brickwork.

After his reception at her offices, Jason decided not to bother with trying to talk his way past the video cameras and security guards that adorned the massive glass doors and long canvas canopy at the front of the building. From across the street, leaning against an ancient palm tree, one of many that lined the wide pavements, he watched the building for some time, Len Furey's script in a slim briefcase under his arm. He watched cars approaching, turning into the ramp and activating the roll-up door to the garage at the bottom by remote control. From the position of the guard and the video surveillance he worked out that there was a blind spot on the left rearside as a car headed down the slope. If he crouched down behind the wing, he wouldn't be seen by the security guard or the video camera or the driver of the car, especially as the sun was now setting rapidly and it was getting dark.

Crossing the road again, he waited behind another palm that screened him from the view of the security guard in the entrance of the building. It was about half an hour before he saw the next car – a big Mercedes S-type salon – turning left across the road, obviously intending to head down the steep ramp. Coming out from behind the tree, Jason timed his walk perfectly, arriving at the brickwork entrance to the ramp at exactly the same moment as the Mercedes, and merrily indicating to the driver, a peroxide blonde woman in her sixties, that she should go first. Smiling broadly and mouthing a thank you, thinking no doubt what a nice young man he was, she drove the big car down the ramp. She didn't notice that the nice young man ducked down behind her rear wing as she pushed the button on her remote control to roll-up the garage door, then pulled the big car into the large basement.

Jason was in. The roll-up door clattered down behind him as he ran off to the side and hunkered down behind a dark blue Rolls Royce Corniche, waiting for the woman to park the Mercedes and find her way to the lift.

As soon as she was gone Jason got to his feet, carefully checking the ceiling for video cameras first. There were none. He walked over to the lift and pressed the call button. This was a very expensive apartment block judging from the cars in the garage – Ferraris, Rolls Royces, Maseratis and Cadillacs, all testament to their owner's wealth.

The lift arrived. Jason vaguely remembered being put into a lift before. He could see Harriet pushing the controls but the panel had had only one button and this had six. Perhaps there was another private lift that lead directly to the penthouse.

On the sixth floor the lift doors opened to reveal a small, heavily carpeted hall, which, besides the lift, had only one door. It was painted a dark burgundy red with three brass mortice locks on one side and a video camera above it. The wide-angle lens encompassed the whole hallway. There was no bell push or door knocker but, oddly, Jason thought he could hear a bell ringing somewhere behind the door, perhaps triggered by the arrival of the lift.

Jason suddenly felt deeply depressed. He hadn't thought this through properly at all. Harriet would undoubtedly have servants. They would answer the door and he would get no further than he'd got at her offices; in fact, they might already have called security or even the police, alerted by his unauthorised arrival in the hallway.

He stood wondering whether he should rap on the door with his knuckles or flee.

'Jason!' The door had been flung open and Cynthia rushed out into the hall, threw herself into his arms and kissed him firmly on the mouth. 'What a surprise, what a great surprise . . . come in, come in . . .' she said, taking his hand and drawing him through the door.

'I . . . ah . . .' It was definitely not the reception he had expected.

RETURN TO THE CASTING COUCH

To say the apartment was sumptuous was an understatement. The floor of the long, wide hallway was tiled in a rare and exquisite marble, its creamy colour striated with streaks of black and a subtle orange. On the walls, lined in silk, were a series of paintings, each lit from an overhead halogen spotlight. There was a Renoir and a Picasso and, a little further down, a Chagall and a Gauguin.

Cynthia led him by the hand into a vast sitting room. One wall was nothing but glass revealing a panorama of most of LA – the lights sparkling out as darkness set, the plumes of fire from the oil rigs out at sea, the most dramatic detail in the huge canvas.

'What a view,' Jason said. The wall of windows led out on to a terrace where Cynthia had clearly been sitting, magazines and a bottle of premier cru Chablis in a silver wine cooler, with one half full glass beside it standing on a white cast-iron table.

'This is so great, Jason... so great,' she said, hugging him again. 'Do you want a drink?'

'That wine looks good.'

'You know Harry, nothing but the best.'

Jason watched her as she waltzed out through the terrace doors. She was wearing a silk satin slip, with spaghetti straps on her slim shoulders and absolutely nothing else. Her hair was cut short and rather spiky, bleached blonde too many times to be soft. She was small and thin, a little waif of a girl, perhaps no more than nineteen but looking much older. It was the penalty she'd paid for the way she had treated herself, allowing herself to be used and abused. In her few short years, she had seen and done things that few would even have imagined. But that was before Harriet had rescued her from the streets. With Harriet's money and care she had come off drugs and no longer had the pressures of life on the game.

The sitting room was as sumptuous as the hall. Its floor was a rich dark oak with Persian rugs strewn over the wood. All the furniture was modern, including two enormous sofas that faced each other, separated by an occasional table that looked as though it was made of a sheet of glass more than two feet thick. On the walls, all carefully lit, there were paintings by Cézanne, Matisse and even a Turner.

Jason was sure, even in his drugged condition, he had never seen the inside of this apartment.

Cynthia tripped back in with the wine cooler. She went to a large bookcase, its glassed-in shelves stacked with rare first editions, and pushed a small lever. The shelves slid noiselessly to one side to reveal a bar with every conceivable bottle of spirit, every type of glass and bottle of wine – the whites and champagne in cooled cabinets – all neatly arranged. Cynthia took a large wineglass and filled it with Chablis.

'There,' she said, handing him the glass and clinking the edge against her own. 'This is great,' she repeated. 'Come on ... this way ...'

Almost before he'd had a chance to taste the wine, she caught his hand and pulled him back into the hall. She opened the door at the far end and led him into a bedroom – another vast room dominated by a huge double bed, its thick carpet a deep red, as were its walls and curtains. The curtains were drawn and Cynthia switched on the lights, dimming them immediately to a pleasant glow.

'Harry thinks of everything ...' Cynthia said

throwing herself on the bed, the slip riding up over her hips. 'Close the door, baby...'

Jason did as he was told, puzzled by her reaction.

'Look...' She pulled open the drawer of the bedside table and extracted a large black dildo. She giggled, 'See, I thought I was going to have to wank tonight.'

She looked at him steadily, mistaking his puzzlement for something else.

'What's the matter, baby? You want something more kinky? I don't mind. Whatever you want... there's the other room...'

'No, no, this is fine, Cyn...'

'Come on then, big boy. Get your clothes off. I remember that cock of yours. Quite an instrument. Harry knew what a good time I had with you. She's so good to me...'

Jason began to cotton on. Cynthia was assuming Harriet had sent Jason over to entertain Cynthia while she was off somewhere. That was why she hadn't asked him how he had got into the building. He debated disillusioning her but decided it would be better to wait until later to tell her the real reason for his visit, especially as she appeared so enthusiastic at the idea Harriet would look after her in this way.

Putting his briefcase and his wine down, Jason pulled off his clothes as Cynthia turned on her stomach, her head in her hands, watching his every move.

'Look at that chest. Nice big muscles. I like that,' she said, giving a running commentary as more was revealed. 'Yeah, I remember those legs...' As he tugged off his boxer shorts, Cynthia rolled over on to her back, twisted round so her feet were at the foot of the bed and opened her legs, letting Jason see her sex.

He had definitely seen that before. Instead of the usual triangle of hair on her belly, her thick wiry and very black curls had been trimmed into a long narrow oval shape covering the hood of her clitoris but not the rest of her labia. 'Going to get myself warmed up...' she said, picking up the dildo and sliding its head into the furrow of her sex until it rested against her clitoris. She twisted the knarled end and a loud humming filled the room.

'Is that good?' Jason asked, naked now.

'Mmm...'

'Do you remember last time?'

'Sure. You've got a great cock, Jason. It's nice to be alone this time though...' She moved the dildo down to the mouth of her sex then pushed it inside. The humming changed to a deeper tone. 'You like to see this?'

Jason tried to concentrate on watching her. He wanted to ask her where Harriet was and when she'd be back. He wanted to ask her about last time, where he'd been and exactly what they'd done. He tried to put both thoughts aside.

'Yes...' he said, watching the dildo move in and out of her sex, its shell coated with her juices already.

'I love people watching me wank,' Cynthia said. She suddenly pushed the dildo right up into her body until only the knarled end was visible. 'Oh...' she moaned.

'That's very deep,' he said.

'Yes...' He saw her wriggling her body against the dildo. 'Do it for me...' she said.

'I'd like that.' He sat on the bed and reached forward to replace her fingers with his on the end of the dildo. He pulled it all the way out, then pushed it back up again. He got on to his knees so he could get to her clitoris with his other hand, probing between her open labia until his forefinger found the tiny nodule of nerves. Gently he wanked it from side to side.

'Oh good, good . . .' Cyn said laying back, completely relaxed.

Jason pushed the vibrator in and out, his finger establishing a regular pattern on her clit, pressing it from side to side with absolute regularity.

'Oh good . . .' she sighed.

He could see her small round breasts under the slip, one of her nipples exposed as it had rucked up. He looked into her eyes but they were not looking at him or anything else. 'You're making me come,' she murmured.

'Good. Come for me. I want to see it. Then I'll fuck you.'

'Umm . . .'

He saw her eyelids flutter, then close and her body shuddered. He felt a spasm, which made her clitoris leap under his finger. She scissored her legs together, trapping his hand and the dildo between her thighs on its upward stroke and shuddered again. This time her whole body was trembling from head to toe as her orgasm seized her. It shook through her, so sudden, so unexpected, the arrival of Jason only minutes before a wonderful surprise. The memory of what they had done to him, how he had been used, had instantly started her sexual pulse. Now it had had its first release, but she still had a long way to go.

She opened her eyes and looked down at his cock. It was sticking up from between his thighs, hard as steel. She slid down the bed towards it, reaching out with one hand to circle it. Then she fed it into her mouth, sucking it eagerly while she sent her other hand round, down his buttocks and into the cleft of his arse. With no hesitation, she found the crater of his anus and thrust her finger inside. It was too dry to get far. Without moving her mouth away, she brought her hand back, dipped her finger into her own liquid sex, making sure it was well coated with her juices, then brought it round again to Jason's arse. This time, as she pushed it into his anus, her finger slid home easily.

She felt his cock react to her penetration. She pushed forward further, trying to get it as deep as it would go, only her knuckles restricting it. At the same time she sucked on his cock with her mouth, sucked it hard and not at all gently.

'Oh . . .' Jason gasped, but not from pain. There *was* pain but that only seemed to heighten the pleasure, to make it more resonant, more profound.

Satisfied she could get her finger no deeper, Cyn began to explore, searching for the little gland that she knew could deliver so much feeling. She felt him contract as she found it, his body shivering, his cock throbbing. Gently she coaxed it, manipulating its sensitivity, trying to judge what was best by the reaction of his cock in the vacuum of her mouth.

'Cyn, Cyn . . .' he groaned, feeling his spunk rising, her finger touching the most sensitive spot in his body.

Jason toppled forward and to one side grabbing Cynthia's thighs, pulling her over on to her back so he could move his mouth down between her legs. He found her clitoris with his tongue. Concentrating on her, on giving her pleasure, was the only way of stopping himself from coming. He felt her shifting around underneath him, then sucking his cock deep, her finger still embedded in his arse.

His tongue lapped out, pushing the oval-shaped hair of her pubis out of the way, searching for the next target. Suddenly, she felt like a molten lake beneath him. Enthusiastically he hoovered up her labia, sucking on them, then releasing them and plunging his tongue as deep as it would go into the centre of her sex.

Now it was her turn to moan.

He brought his hands up under her thighs, feeling for the entrance to her rear passage, just as she'd felt for his. Finding it, wet from the juice that had run down between her legs, he penetrated it without hesitation pushing one finger, then two, as deep as they would go, as deep as her finger was buried in him. Almost unintentionally his other two fingers, sliding around on her wet labia, slipped into her cunt.

'My god...' she said. He could feel the sound waves vibrating his cock, her mouth momentarily loosened. He felt her body shudder under him.

He wriggled all four fingers in her body as his tongue went to find her clitoris, this time licking it with long strokes, his tongue rough and hot. He felt her sex contract on his hand.

She was using her hand not only to penetrate his anus, but to push him forward, to force his cock deeper into her mouth, so deep he could feel her throat and wondered how she managed not to gag. At the same time, how he did not know, her finger had managed to close on his little oval-shaped gland, massaging where he could never remember feeling a finger before, and driving him wild with the new sensations. It was as though the finger wasn't inside his arse at all, but was in his cock, probing and prodding the part of his body that was solely responsible for making him come. If she continued like this, nothing he could do would stop it.

'No,' he said, sitting up and pulling her finger from his body, like a knife drawn from a sheath. 'I don't want that.'

'Oh let me. I love the taste of spunk.' Cyn looked disappointed.

'I'll give you spunk.'

'Like this then . . .' she said, rolling over and getting on all fours, sticking her small but very round bum out at him. 'Like this . . .'

He wasn't sure whether she meant for him to bugger her or take her from behind. He swung round and knelt between her legs.

'What do you want?'

'Everything,' she said unhelpfully, her voice husky and deep.

He knew what *he* wanted. He wanted her cunt. He wanted her heat and wetness. Pushing forward, he nosed his shaft between her labia. She thrust her buttocks back at him and his cock slid into the liquid core he had created, up and up until he could feel the neck of her womb against his glans.

'Oh yes . . . so big, such a big boy . . .'

Cynthia wriggled her arse from side to side. Jason could still feel the impression her finger had left in his anus, a feeling he could increase by squeezing his buttocks together.

'Have you got spunk for me? A nice load of come . . .'

she said, looking over her shoulder at him, her eyes bright.

Holding her slim hips, Jason looked down her narrow back, her buttocks nudging against his navel, her thin legs parted. She put her head down, her spiky blonde hair even more dishevelled now, and looked between her legs to see his cock penetrating her. He felt her cunt contract.

'Come on, give it to me. I want it...'

And he wanted it too. She had almost made him come in her mouth. He was more than ready.

Slowly he withdrew then pushed forward again, wanting to build slowly, knowing that was what made him come most strongly. After everything he had been through in his time in Hollywood, he knew his body well by now, knew what pleased it, what was best for it.

'Oh, what a fucking great cock...' Cyn gasped. 'I love it, I love it. I love cock. I love to eat it. I love to fuck it. I love it in my arse. Are you going to spunk me, big boy? Are you going to give me all that lovely juice? Are you going to let me have it, right up my cunt. Can you feel how wet I am for you?'

As he pushed forward, he felt something against his knee. It was the black vibrator. He picked it up.

'Come on big boy... I'm hungry for it...' Cyn said as his rhythm stopped. She looked over her shoulder to see what he was doing. 'Yes... yes...' she said, seeing the vibrator in his hand.

He put the head of the dildo against the little puckered bud of her anus, withdrawing his cock almost to the lips of her sex. In this position he could see his cock poised, looking as though it were being kissed by her labia and, above it, the mouth of her anus like a crater of the moon turned inside out.

He pushed the dildo forward, watching as Cyn relaxed her muscles and he slid it in. He pushed again and he slid deeper.

'Two cocks, oh that's so great...'

He thrust his cock back into her cunt. The architecture of it had been changed completely by the dildo. One side was hard and unyielding pressing against his shaft. He turned the knarled knob at the end of the black phallus and felt an instant vibration coursing though her sex and his own, the head of the vibrator right up against his glans. Cyn moaned.

Jason pulled back, then thrust forward again. As the end of the dildo was pressed against his navel it too was plunged deeper into Cyn's body.

'Two cocks,' she moaned. 'Oh I love it... love it. Are you going to spunk me, big boy? I need your spunk...'

The vibrations on his cock were making it difficult to hold back. He looked down at her buttocks, the cleft bisected by the dildo, its black shaft sliding in and out with the movement of his body. As he pushed forward, ramming his cock right up into her hot wet sex, the dildo thrust forward too, filling her arse, the vibrations increased by the constriction and proximity, two phalluses reaming into a girl so slight of build she didn't look as if she'd be able to take one.

She hadn't stopped talking for one moment, a stream of obscenities, begging him to suck her and bugger her and use her. 'Oh I'd like to get one of my friends to lick your balls, lick your arse, get her tongue right up inside you, rub her tits all over your back. Come on, fuck me, fuck me...' It was meant to turn him on, but it turned her on too. He felt her body beginning to tremble, felt her sex contracting around his cock, heard her voice falter as the orgasm robbed her of the ability to make coherent sounds. 'Get your... spunk... cock... my arse... spunk...'

He felt her wriggle back on him at the same moment he thrust forward, wanting and getting that last inch of penetration. And then she stopped, her whole body rigid, every muscle locked, as she looked down between her legs one final time, seeing Jason's balls hanging down from her labia. Then she came, her eyes forced shut, another orgasm stretching her taut like an electric shock, her sex contracting around the shaft of his cock, so fiercely it felt like she could feel its every contour. It went on and on and on, refusing to release her, her body caught in its spell, every muscle she possessed locked solid, impossible to think of anything else but the two phalluses buried inside her.

Jason couldn't move. His cock was trapped inside her as if embedded in steel.

Slowly she relaxed, her body melting over him, a sensation like a flower opening in bright sunlight. The head of his cock was surrounded by molten, silky flesh.

He pulled back, slid the dildo out of her body, then thrust forward again, not wanting the hard plastic next to him. He felt her sex folding around him on all sides, its core seeming to suck him in. He wouldn't have to thrust again. His glans had found its special place, a place lined with the finest silk, a place that seemed to be caressing it, coaxing it, provoking it to spunk, the rest of his cock held firm, but his glans open and free.

'Spunk me, big boy,' Cyn said quietly.

And he did. He felt his spunk gush out into her

special place, strings of white-hot spunk lashing into the centre of her. As he did, he thought he felt it respond, almost as though it were kissing him, sucking him in, drawing the spunk out of him . . .

They sat out on the terrace. Cynthia had opened a bottle of Louis Roederer Cristal, set in a silver wine cooler on a Georgian silver tray with two Baccarat crystal champagne flutes. She had dressed her slender body in a pair of black lace trousers with a matching long-sleeved blouse, its length abbreviated to finish just under her breasts, leaving a gap of naked flesh above the waist of the trousers. She wore no underwear and the semi-transparent lace gave glimpses of her unusually shaped pubic hair and her small pert breasts.

'You want something to eat?' she asked as they sipped the champagne.

He shook his head.

'That was great, Jason . . . so great . . .' She sat on one of the comfortable deeply cushioned chairs with her feet up on the white table, little black satin mules with high heels balanced precariously on her toes. 'I can't get over Harry thinking of it. What a great surprise . . .' 'Great' seemed to be Cynthia's favourite word.

'She didn't,' Jason said, deciding it was time for the truth.

'What?'

'She didn't. I mean, Harry didn't send me round here.'

'She didn't?'

'No. I sneaked in through the garage and up in the lift.'

'Really. Why didn't you just ask the doorman to let you in?'

'I didn't think Harry would want to see me.'

Cynthia laughed. 'I would have...'

'That's what I thought.'

'And I thought it was Harry's idea.' She looked slightly crestfallen but brightened up immediately. 'Well, I'm sure Harry would have done it if she thought about it. I mean, she doesn't mind me having men. Look who I'm telling that... You saw for yourself...'

'Yes,' Jason said, though he wasn't at all sure what he'd seen last time.

'So why did you come? You didn't want to see me?'

'Of course, Cyn. But I though Harry would be here too.'

'She would have been. But she got called away late this afternoon. And she'll be gone a week. That's why I thought...'

'Where's she gone?'

'Business. She never tells me. Knows I'm not really interested. Why did you want to see her?'

'Long story.'

'Tell me,' she sipped her wine. With her feet up Jason could see the lace crotch of the trousers and underneath it part of her labia.

'You really want to know?'

'Sure.'

So he told her. He started at the beginning and told her about Hanna bringing him over to LA to star in *The Casting Couch*, how she'd shared him out among her friends and that, finally, when he'd confronted her, they'd had a flaming row and she had thrown him out of the house, calling everyone in Hollywood to tell them not to touch him with a bargepole. He told her about Nancy and Camilla and making *Escape of the Whores*. He didn't mention how cross he had been about being drugged and given to Harriet Teitelbaum for a command performance with Cyn.

'Gee . . .' Cynthia said when he'd finished. She sipped her champagne. 'And I thought you knew.'

'Knew what?'

'I mean with Harry, that night . . . I thought it had all been arranged. You didn't, did you?'

'The night you brought me here?'

'Hanna's provided a lot of guys. I just thought you were one of them.'

'I didn't know anything. Hanna just told me I had to go with you. Then she put something in my drink . . .'

'To loosen you up.'

'It certainly did that.'

'See, Harry knows I like it. Don't get me wrong, I get off with her all the time. She ain't pretty or any of that but boy she can turn me on. She's into all sorts of things and I got to tell you she's got me into them too. I mean, before I met her I turned tricks with women but I never got into it. Now it drives me crazy. But she knows I want men too. I could never give up cock. So we have these little sessions and Harry arranges to have them filmed. I get fucked and a lot of other stuff and then we watch it later in bed and we both get turned on. She's the kind of dike who wishes she had a cock, so seeing some guy giving me a porcupine is like . . . well, guess she wishes it was her. She straps on a dildo and does exactly what he does on screen . . .'

Jason finished his glass of champagne, took the bottle out of the cooler, refilling his own glass and

Cynthia's. The night air was balmy and there was a scent of flowers from a jasmine that grew from a pot on the terrace and up over the window frame. Below, the lights of Los Angeles lay in a more or less regular grid.

'I don't remember much about it. I certainly don't remember this apartment...'

'No. We took you down to the basement. There's another elevator. Strictly private. There's a little studio down there, like a theatre. It's got a big two-way glass wall. People can watch.'

'Watch?'

'Yeah. I mean you can't see them but they can see you. It turns me on, knowing there's people watching me...'

There was obviously very little that didn't turn Cynthia on.

'We were being watched?' Another part of Jason's memory clicked into place. He remembered the strange appearance of one of the walls in the room.

'Sure.'

'And Hanna does this regularly?'

'What?'

'Provides boys... men.'

'Oh yeah, but not like you, Jason. You're special, special special. I can't wait to see the film.'

'I didn't want to do it.'

'I'll watch it with Harry. She thought you were great too.'

'She wouldn't see me this afternoon.'

'What, you went to the office?'

'This afternoon.'

'Oh, that don't mean anything. She never sees

anyone like that. You still haven't told me what you wanted to see her for, anyway?'

Jason walked back into the living room, where he had left his briefcase, and took out the script. He brought it back to the terrace and put it on the table in front of Cynthia. Putting her feet down, she picked the blue-bound pages and flicked through them while Jason explained what it was.

'Helen Talbot suggested I get in touch with Harriet.'

'Helen ... ahh. Did you meet Honey?'

'More than meet.'

'I bet.'

'She told me you used to be' – he was going to say hookers but changed it to – 'friends.'

'Yeah, she was always into women though. She was even with Harry for a while. It's a small town, Jason.'

'Seems like it.'

He wanted to pursue the subject of the script but wasn't at all sure it was a good idea. He had the feeling that Harriet compartmentalised her life, that Cynthia was in one compartment labelled enjoyment and sex, and everything to do with business was in another, the two never mixing. He didn't want the script to get stuck in Cynthia's box.

'How long have you been with her?' he asked, changing the subject.

'Two years. I was in big trouble. I was into coke in a big way, turning tricks on Hollywood Boulevard to pay for the stuff. Jesus, I felt ill all the time. She was just cruising by in her big stretch looking for pussy for one of her little basement shows. Wanted me to be fucked by two guys while she watched with whoever her girlfriend was then. Well afterwards, when she paid me off, she was looking at me all funny, you know almost motherly like... The rest is history...'

For a moment the conversation lapsed. They sat in silence looking out over the spread of the city down below, the straight lines of the streetlights, the bright neons decorating the taller buildings, a million sparkling lights. It was a stark contrast to the total blackness of the ocean beyond, a yawning black chasm, lit only by the gas burners of the oil platforms far out to sea.

'So...' Cynthia said emphatically.

'So?'

'We've got to do something about this script, haven't we? You want Harry to put up the money right?'

'Yes, but I...'

'Are you hungry?'

He hadn't thought about it, but suddenly Jason was starving. 'Yes.'

'Good. Go find the kitchen. There's a number by the phone. Order up a couple of pizzas and I'll read it while I'm waiting. Tell them it's for me. They know what I like.'

'Read it now...'

'Sure, I know I look as though I can't read squat. It's all right. I'm used to it. People think I'm stupid...'

'I didn't...'

'Last hit Harry had, I found. I read every script she's going to do now. If I don't like it, it don't get done, simple as that... Go on, order the pizza...'

As Jason headed indoors Cynthia got up from the table, filled her champagne glass and carried it over to one of the big loungers on the terrace. With the champagne on a little table by her elbow, she made herself comfortable, took a pair of glasses from a bag, and put them on before opening the script. The glasses, oval lenses with red frames, changed her face completely, making her look serious and rather plain.

Finding the kitchen, Jason called the number pinned to the wall by the phone. Whether he liked it or not, Cynthia was involved now. All he could do was hope what she said was true, and not just an illusion Harriet Teitelbaum liked to encourage to make her feel important. If it was the latter then he didn't think much of the chances of Harriet's reaction being positive.

Coming back into the living room, he watched Cynthia through the patio doors, her knees raised, the script resting on them as she read. There was nothing he could do now but wait.

Chapter Five

Some mornings in Los Angeles were grim, the smog in the valley held in by high atmospheric pressure, never escaping the hills that surrounded the city on three sides and made worse by the morning rush hour. The air was thick and gritty, tasting foul, and the blue sky could only be seen through a filter of grime. But this morning a wind had cleared the pollution away, filled the air with ionised ozone from the sea, and made the sky the brightest of blues, the few clouds that straggled by so white they looked as though they had been made of cotton wool.

Jason sat in Nancy's small, lavishly planted garden, sharing coffee and waffles with her before she went to work at the theatrical agency where he had first met her. It had been late by the time he had got home last night and she was already asleep. Nancy slept like she did everything else – deeply and enthusiastically – so Jason's news had had to wait until the morning.

As they drank coffee he told her everything that had happened last night, holding nothing back, not the fact Cynthia had thought he was a surprise package from Harriet, nor the details of their sex, or the explanation of what had occurred on his previous visit which Nancy knew had puzzled him. He told her everything Cynthia had said, glad to have it clear in his own mind.

Nancy listened to all this with interest. She had told him from the beginning of their relationship that she did not expect him to be faithful to her. It would be totally hypocritical, she'd explained, if, after getting so much enjoyment from his performances on camera with other women, she objected to him doing the same thing in reality. He knew, of course, that it turned her on. Nancy loved sex. She was very good at it, with a voluptuous and eager body, but part of her sexuality was a strong desire to watch. She had watched him avidly on video and it had doubled her pleasure as he'd made love to her. Listening to his account of what he had done with Cynthia – and before that his encounter with Helen and Honey – gave her the same kind of thrill.

'Anyway . . .' he concluded as she finished her coffee, '. . . she read the script and thinks it's great.'

'Really?'

'She's going to give it to Harriet as soon as she gets back. She said it was the best thing she's ever read.'

'One out of one,' Nancy said.

'Bitchy.'

'No, just honest.'

'Wrong. She reads everything Harry is thinking of doing.'

'Really?'

'So she says.'

'You do surprise me. Hey, look at the time, I've got to fly.'

Nancy stood up. Her strong, powerful body was clad in a dark green suit, its skirt short enough to expose most of her Lycra-clad thighs, the very sheer material shimmering in the sunlight, her high heels shaping her calves and the lush curves of her arse. Her breasts pushed firmly through her white blouse. Her long black hair was pinned to her head making her look very business-like.

'What a pity,' Jason said as he looked at her, knowing she was excited by his story. He reached forward and ran his hand between her thighs. The short skirt rode up and he saw a triangle of black silky nylon under the tights. His fingers stroked her crotch. Even through the two layers of material he could feel she was damp.

'See what you've done,' she said, squeezing his hand slightly with her big thigh muscles.

'I hope it'll keep.'

'You better be stripped for action when I get home.'

'Is that what you want?'

'You can tell me the whole story again. I think I've got a black dildo . . .'

'Action replay . . .'

'Exactly.'

He thought he felt her labia throbbing against his hand as she pulled away, bending to kiss him on the cheek, her big breasts visible under her blouse, held firmly by a white lace bra that emphasised her natural cleavage.

'Bye.'

Jason heard the distinctive sound of Nancy's Volkswagen Beetle pulling away from the house. He poured himself another cup of coffee from the thermos pot Nancy used and turned his face into the sun, putting his feet up on the table.

If Cynthia had been sincere in what she had said about the script — and Jason knew enough about Hollywood by now not to take that for granted — and Harriet Teitelbaum really did take her advice about what projects she should invest in, then his visit had been a success. He did not particularly like the idea of being involved with Harriet, especially as he now knew precisely what had been done to him the night he had been taken there. He had no doubt he would be required to perform again with Cyn in the basement 'theatre' if she did put up the money, but that was a price he was willing to pay if it meant Len Furey's film would be made.

On the other hand, of course, Cynthia's influence might be purely illusory. Harriet Teitelbaum had made a great deal of money and had done it, Jason supposed, without the advice of a nineteen-year-old ex-prostitute and drug addict. Cynthia's abilities and talents in the bedroom were obviously attractive to Harry but that did not mean she was prepared to listen to a word Cyn said on any other subject. She might humour her, coax her into thinking she was making a contribution but, in fact, not take a blind bit of notice of what she said.

Jason's elation at Cynthia's reaction to the script died as he remembered all the reservations he had had last night. The more he considered it, the more likely it was that Harriet merely let Cyn think she was important to her business plans but actually paid no attention to her at all. He had gone around to see Harriet, not Cynthia, to give Harriet the script, following Helen Talbot's advice. Now, whatever happened, the project was inextricably tied up in the intricacies of Harriet's relationship with Cynthia, and that might be a very bad thing.

Getting more depressed by the moment, Jason reviewed his options. If luck had closed his route to Harriet and barring Len Furey finding the money for himself – which he had not done so far – Jason's options were very limited. He certainly didn't want to stay in LA if his future was making more porno films – however enjoyable the experience had been in purely physical terms. Neither did he want to return to England with his tail between his legs.

There was one other possibility, of course, one other faint hope. He looked at his watch. It was too late today but tomorrow he'd set the alarm and get up early. He smiled to himself. Getting up early was exactly what he would have to do.

The taxi dropped him a little way from the electrically controlled gates of Hanna Silverstein's Beverly Hills mansion. There was no way through the high metal fencing at the front but, when he had lived in the house, Jason had noticed that alongside the driveway, where it opened out into a brick-laid courtyard in front of the garage complex, a long way from the main house, the fencing had come away from its support at the corner of the brickwork. Slowly and carefully, keeping his head well down so he couldn't be seen from the mansion windows, Jason worked his way along the outside of the fencing, hiding under a row of shrubs. To his relief, he found that the wire at the far end was still flapping loose. He did not know of course, that the moment he'd stepped off the road, his presence was registered on the electronic security system and followed by video camera . . .

Squeezing through the gap in the thickly meshed wire, Jason walked around the garage and up the long sloping lawn to the main house. During his days here Hanna had got up early every morning to swim in the full-sized pool that was beautifully landscaped into the terrace at the back of the house. It was a routine he'd never known her to miss.

Coming up through a thick bank of rhododendron, he silently edged his way to a vantage point overlooking the pool. There was no sign of Hanna. He looked at his watch and settled down to wait, making sure he was well hidden.

No more than ten minutes later, Hanna Silverstein appeared in a white satin robe, a big white bath towel over her arm. She put the towel on the back of one of the terrace chairs and stripped off the robe to reveal a very functional black single-piece swimsuit. Draping the robe over the chair too, Hanna took three little running steps and dived into the pool, the movement so practised and graceful, her body position so perfect, arms extended, hands together, that she seemed to slice into the water, hardly disturbing it at all. She began ploughing up and down the length of the pool, her stroke as perfect as her dive, the surface of the water barely troubled – like a fish, Hanna was in her element. She had told Jason she almost swam for the US Olympic team in her teens and the daily swim always seemed to leave her, temporarily at least, in a relaxed and propitious mood, her natural affinity with the water a pleasure that did not require her to impose her will upon the world.

Jason watched as she swam up and down using the front crawl, her spin turns at each end accurately and seemingly effortless, the push off from the side of the pool so strong she was propelled underwater, her body stretched like a blade, for a considerable distance before another stroke was necessary to maintain her momentum.

After fifty lengths she pulled herself from the water, not bothering using the steps at the side of the pool.

This was the moment he had been waiting for. With no idea what her reaction would be Jason got to his feet and walked down on to the terrace.

'Good morning,' he said.

'Hi, Jason,' she said. If she was surprised to see him she didn't show it. She picked up the towel and started drying her hair.

'Good swim?'

'You know it's always wonderful for me.' Her voice was soft and gentle, not at all like her more normal, strident tone. 'It's nice to see you.'

'Is it?'

'Sure. I always liked you, Jason.' She held out her hand for him to come closer, then took hold of his. 'Really liked,' she added, squeezing it.

'I liked you too,' he said. It was not entirely untrue. In this mood, the cares of the world washed away by the water, Hanna was a different person. She even looked different, her face relaxed, unfurrowed, making her appear younger.

She pulled him closer to her, then stroked his face with her other hand. 'So pretty,' she said.

'Thank you.'

'You make me want you,' she said, her fingers moving around to the back of his neck and massaging it hard. 'Will you take me to bed?'

'That would be nice,' he said lamely. It was working out better than he'd expected. 'In the study?' he asked. Hanna had a private room just off the terrace. She'd taken him there in this gentle mood.

'No ... upstairs ...'

There was an edge in the way she said it and the flicker of an expression in her eyes that Jason could not read, but he put it down to her surprise at suddenly seeing him appear out of the blue. Leading him by the hand, she took him through the house, up the curved staircase in the main hall and along to her bedroom, the room where he had slept while he was living in the house. The white silk sheets of the large double bed were ruffled, the thin quilt half on the floor.

'You came at the right time. I'm in the mood for this. Do you know that? Really in the mood,' Hanna said as soon as the bedroom door was closed. 'Take my swimsuit off, darling.'

She stood by the bed while he obediently pulled the shoulder straps down her arms then eased the bust off, revealing her small breasts, her comparatively big nipples hardened by the water. He wriggled it over her hips until it was around her thighs, and then it fell, of its own accord, to the floor. She stepped out of it, leaving it on the floor, and began to unbutton Jason's shirt.

'We had some good times, didn't we?' she said.

'Yes.'

'You gave me a good time.'

'It was mutual.'

'I get all excited just thinking about what you did to me.'

She had unbuttoned the shirt and the top of his jeans, sliding her hand into his fly and groping around for his cock. She found it already growing in his boxer shorts, gathered it into her fist and squeezed it hard.

'That's what I want.'

She lay back on the bed and watched as he stripped off the rest of his clothes, opening her legs slightly and stroking the thin wispy blond pubic hair very gently, as if petting some delicate little animal.

Jason, his cock unfurling rapidly, sat on the bed beside her and caressed her slender thighs. There were a lot of things he wanted to say to her, all the things he'd rehearsed over and over again, the reasons he'd taken the chance of coming, but he thought if he launched into it now her mood might be destroyed.

His hand reached up to her breasts, cupping the nearest in his palm and feeling her hard, cold nipple under it. He rubbed it aggressively and Hanna moaned. His cock reacted too, swiftly ripening to full maturity. His hand went to the other breast, using his fingers to pinch its nipple while he bent forward to apply his tongue to the first, lapping around it then biting it teasingly. He licked all over her breasts, up to her slender neck, over her throat, then down again, down over her navel, licking, then kissing, then nibbling her flesh until his tongue was nuzzling into the blonde hair at the triangle of her belly.

She opened her legs wider and took her own hand away. He licked over to one side, on to her hip, then followed the crease between leg and pelvis, down to the apex of her thighs, then up again along the other side. Hanna moaned, her hands behind her head, lifting it so she could watch what he was doing.

Jason's mouth centred on her sex now, his tongue having little trouble parting the wispy hair to get between her labia. He moved the rest of his body into a kneeling position besides her, the head of his cock tucked against his own navel.

He moved both hands down under her thighs, so he could nestle his fingers into the mouth of her sex while his tongue found the nut of her clitoris.

'Oh, Jason... It's good to have you back... so good...'

He could feel her body react as he licked the familiar swollen bud of nerves. He was not gentle, letting his tongue stroke against it strongly, before concentrating on the very top of it, using the tip of his tongue to push it to and fro, which he knew she loved.

'You'll make me come...'

He didn't stop. Instead he made sure this tiny movement was absolutely regular, like a metronome, so she could rely on it, build on it, each caress racking up the tension in her body, higher and higher, until she was bound to fall.

'Don't stop... don't stop...' she said unnecessarily, knowing he wouldn't.

The movement was perfect, just the exact amount of pressure, just the right place, just the ideal tempo to and fro. Hanna let her body go, let herself go, let herself be taken over by her sexual pulse, let her orgasm sweep over her, her mind stoking its heat with thoughts of what she knew was yet to come.

Feeling her orgasm run its course, Jason lifted his head from between her legs and looked up at her.

'You were always good at that.'

Without replying he began to swing himself on top of her body.

'No,' she said quickly. 'Let me.' She sat up, using her elbows for support. Her hands indicated that he should lay flat on his back. 'Let me...' she repeated.

He lay flat, his cock lying ready on his navel, its head almost reaching his bellybutton. Hanna came up to her knees and took his phallus in both her hands, gripping it fiercely, liking to feel its hardness, wanking it slowly at the same time. A tear of fluid had developed at its tip. She leant forward and licked it away with her tongue.

'Put your arms out, stretched out,' she said. 'I want to tie you down.'

'What?' She had never suggested anything like that before.

'Shh... let me, darling. I want it. I was so turned on when I saw it in the film... when Mandy sat on your face. I want to try it.' She squeezed his cock as if to encourage him.

Jason hesitated, but only for a moment. He certainly didn't want to destroy Hanna's good humour by refusing, not considering it had got him this far.

Her hands left his cock. She stretched his arms up above his head, then crawled up the bed to the corner and reached down below the level of the mattress, coming up with a padded leather cuff attached to a nylon rope. She slipped the cuff over Jason's wrist and buckled it in place. In seconds she had repeated the process with the other arm, stretching his arms wide apart above his head.

Hanna got up off the bed and looked down at him.

'God, I love that, seeing you like this,' she said.

Clearly, Jason's body was equally enthusiastic, his cock hard and hot, twitching visibly under her stare.

There were cuffs attached to the corners of the foot of the bed too. If they had been there when he was sleeping in the house, he'd never noticed, though he had never looked either. Perhaps Hanna had put them there ready for the opportunity to enact the scene from *Escape of the Whores* with some other lover. It really didn't matter, Jason told himself as Hanna pulled his left ankle down and out towards the corner of the bed and wrapped the leather cuff around it. Walking around the bottom of the bed, she soon had his right ankle secured too. Apparently not quite satisfied she came up to the head of the bed and tightened the rope that held the cuff on his left wrist, making him strain against all the other ropes more tautly in the process.

'Oh, that's so sexy,' she said coming to sit on the bed next to him, her hand snaking across to his nipple until her fingernail could pinch it. The nails left two crescent shapes in his flesh.

'Does it feel good?'

'Yes . . .' he said, with doubt in his voice.

'I love it, there's something about it. You're so helpless. So dependent. Doesn't it make you feel needy?'

'I need to be fucked,' he said truthfully, his cock providing adequate testimony to that fact.

'Oh yes . . . I'm sure you do.'

Her hand pinched his other nipple, then worked its way down to his rampant erection. With her thumb and forefinger she pinched his glans, making it whiten. Jason moaned.

'So vulnerable . . . I never knew I wanted this before I saw that scene . . .'

'Fuck me.'

'Yes, I think I will.'

She knelt up on the bed and swung her leg over his hips so she was kneeling above him, her labia no more than an inch away from his cock.

'I'm so excited, Jason. My cunt is soaking wet. You see I know what I'm going to get now...'

She lowered herself until he could feel the heat of her labia. Then she took his cock in her hand and guided it to the mouth of her sex.

'You want it, don't you?'

'Don't tease me.'

She laughed. 'Why not?'

He tried to arch his hips off the bed to push his cock up into her, but she rose too, not allowing him any further past the wet lips that barely touched him.

'Naughty,' she scolded.

Very, very gently she bounced her body up and down on him, his cock nudging in and out of the first inch of her cunt, never any further, up and down, just enough to give him the feel of her heat and wetness without any real penetration. It was the ultimate frustration, so near and yet so far.

'Please...' he found himself saying, as though he hadn't had sex for weeks.

'Yes, beg me... come on beg me...'

'Please, please, give it to me. Fuck me... please...'

'I like to hear men beg,' she said.

Suddenly, with no warning, she dropped on him, her whole weight forcing his cock into her like a dagger, reaming into her hard as a bone, impaling itself in her body. She gasped as she felt it stabbing against her womb. Then she used all her muscles to squeeze it tightly, wanting to feel exactly how hard it was.

She looked down at his face smiling broadly. She had him exactly where she wanted him. Her little plan had worked out perfectly, considering she had had so little time to prepare. Of course, she had heard the alarm as soon as he started up the drive. She'd focused the security camera on him. There had been plenty of time to make the arrangements before she went down to the pool where she knew he would be waiting for her.

'Poor boy . . .' she said. 'I've got you now, haven't I? Got you where I want you.' She said it loudly.

It was his cue. He had been waiting in the bathroom as Hanna had told him to. He opened the bathroom door as soon as he heard the words and stepped into the bedroom. He was naked and already erect, his fat circumcised cock glistening with the oil he had slobbered over it. The bottle was still in his hand.

'He's a big boy,' he said when he got to the bed, looking down at Jason.

'What is this?' Jason protested, struggling to get up but making no impression on the bonds that held him to the bed.

'Shh . . .' Hanna said. 'This is a friend of mine. Say hello to Al.'

'Hi, fella,' Al said cheerily. He was a big man, a broad chest with muscles so well defined it was obvious he was into weight training. He was blond too, like Jason, his hair so long it reached his shoulders but, apart from the blond hair around his cock, the rest of his body was smooth and hairless, his legs looking as though they had been shaved. There was something familiar about his face and Jason was sure he'd seen him before.

Without waiting to be told, Al knelt on the bed behind Hanna and squeezed more oil from the bottle on to his hands. He transferred this to Hanna's buttocks rubbing it into the cleft of her arse. She gave a little mew of pleasure, squirming herself down on Jason's cock.

'Let me up,' Jason said, his voice cold and determined.

'Jason,' Hanna said quietly. 'Just do this for me. I want it. Do you get that? I want it.'

He looked into her eyes. They were hard and unyielding, her excitement as obvious as her determination to make him bend to her will.

He could have refused to cooperate. Even tied as he was he could have bucked her off him, twisted and fought and made it impossible for her to continue. But if he did that he knew his fragile relationship with Hanna would be over for good. What Hanna Silverstein wanted, Hanna Silverstein got and he was trapped again, trapped by her power, power she had every intention of exercising.

Al was pouring a stream of oil down between her buttocks now. Jason felt it trickling on to his balls.

'Got a nice big cock, has he?' Al asked, kissing her neck. She turned her head around so he could kiss her mouth, a long lingering kiss, his oily hands going under her arms to clasp her breasts. Jason watched as his strong fingers kneaded Hanna's tits, then rubbed the nipples between his thumb and forefinger as if he were rolling a cigarette. He felt her sex throb, contracting around his cock.

'Umm . . .' Hanna muttered as she broke the kiss and turned back to look down at Jason. 'Do I get what I want?'

Jason had no need to answer. Despite his situation and his anger, the presence of Al had not diminished his excitement. If anything, it had increased it. He knew what was going to happen. It was not something he'd ever experienced before, but the thought aroused him more and more.

Hanna could feel it, could feel the hardness of his throbbing shaft. She rested both her hands on his chest.

'Very sensitive nipples, I remember,' she said, moving her fingers up to pinch them both with her pink-varnished fingernails.

He looked into her eyes. Knowing she was going to get what she wanted, the look of determination had gone; now all he could see was wild unrestrained excitement. He could feel it too, her whole body quivering, her sex juicing and alive.

She dug her fingernails into his nipples and felt his cock kick inside her. The feeling made her spasm too. She wriggled down on him pressing his balls into her bottom, wanting to feel every inch of him. Al's hands were rubbing her breasts, tracing circles on them, pressing her nipples into her chest with the palm of his hands, the oil making the movement feel deliciously sensual. She wallowed in the sensation, but it was not all physical. She loved the feeling of power too, of what she could get men to do for her, because she was who she was.

She felt Al's big hot cock nudging into her buttocks. She threw her head back at right angles to her spine so she could rest her cheek against his.

'You know what I want,' she said unnecessarily. She had told him exactly what she wanted as they watched Jason sneaking up the drive.

'And I'm going to give it to you, baby. Can't you feel how hard I am?'

'All greasy...'

Al's oily-smooth cock dipped down into the chasm of her buttocks. She eased herself off Jason slightly to get in the right position, her whole body knotted with anticipation, as she felt the well-greased glans slip into the corrugated crater of her anus. She wanted it so badly, two cocks filling her, fucking her, possessing her, though the truth was it was she who possessed them.

'Do it,' she said impatiently.

Al's hands left her breasts and slid down to hold her hips, gripping them tightly as his cock centred on the target. Hanna tried to relax her muscles wanting him to be able to penetrate deeply at the first stroke.

'Do it,' she repeated more urgently.

Al bucked his hips and his cock surged forward into her rear. The first stroke took him halfway in, the second all the way, right up into her, until his shaft was buried in her tight, hot arse, the passage made even narrower, even more constricted, by the presence of Jason's cock in her cunt.

'God ... god ...' Hanna screamed, the wave of pain at this first intrusion doubled by his second, the pain overwhelming her, but turning, by some internal equation, to instant unbelievable pleasure. It rolled her eyes back in their sockets and in the blackness she saw a vision of the two cocks buried inside her. She didn't need movement, the incredible feeling of being completely filled, penetrated and stuffed with throbbing, hard flesh was enough. She felt every nerve in her body pulse, an electric shock of sensation assailing her, its current joining all her nerves in an arc of excitement that flashed through her body like a blue flame, wringing her dry of everything but its own impact.

As it died she felt Jason start to move. She opened her eyes and looked down at him as he arched his body against his bonds, pushing his cock up into her sex.

'Yes...' she encouraged.

He didn't want her encouragement. He didn't want anything but to come. He was angry and disgusted with himself, disgusted at his own excitement. He wanted to come, he wanted to spunk so badly it almost hurt. He had never felt his balls so full, his whole body aching for release. He had never felt this, another cock, hot and throbbing alongside his, separated only by the membranes of a woman's body.

Wildly he hammered into her, his strokes penetrating deeper and deeper, constantly trying to force his way up, her sex narrow and tight.

'Give it to me, baby,' she cried loudly.

It was then Al started moving too. As Jason withdrew so Al pushed forward, and vice versa, filling the vacant space. At first it was uneven and ragged, a clumsy ballet. But it took only seconds for a rhythm to form.

'Yes, oh god, yes!' Hanna screamed, her body spasming, her fingers clutching at Jason's chest, her long nails raking his flesh rather like a drowning man clutching for a piece of jetsam to keep afloat.

'Yes, yes, yes...' She screamed the words so loud they vibrated round the room. This is exactly what she wanted, two cocks invading her body, splitting her in two, her mind unable to think of anything but the way they pounded into her.

She was coming again, a different kind of orgasm from the first, longer and harder, each piston stroke of cock taking her higher, so high she didn't think she would be able to feel anymore, but she did, until she reached the final pinnacle then crashed down like a house of cards, the images in her mind barely having caught up with the sensations in her body.

Al was coming too, the tightness of her rear passage, the way it had moulded itself to him, the way it seemed to suck the spunk out of his cock, and the feeling of another cock right next to him, impossible to resist.

'I'm coming,' he whispered into Hanna's ear as he felt his cock begin to jerk. He thrust into her one final time but Jason did not stop. Relentlessly he hammered on, hammering against Al's spunking shaft, feeling it climax and not wanting to feel it all at the same time.

Jason's mind refused to work. He didn't want to think about what he was feeling, didn't want to admit he had felt what he had felt, and that it was this sensation that had pushed him to the brink and then over it. He pistoned into Hanna's sex, her wetness making his cock slick, emptying his mind of everything, trying to make it blank, wanting only his release. He struggled at the bonds that held him to the bed as a way of telling himself this had all been forced on him, that it was not his fault. Still pounding in and out of her, he felt his spunk shoot out of his cock. He didn't stop. He pounded faster, harder, deeper, ramming his spunk into her, wanting the orgasm to free him but not wanting its pleasure.

Exhausted and spent, Jason lay with his eyes closed. He felt Hanna climbing off him.

'Go get some breakfast,' he heard her say.

'Sure,' Al said. There was the sound of a kiss and of the bedroom door opening then closing again.

He felt Hanna sit on the side of the bed.

'You bitch. You used me again. Every time I see you, you use me,' he wanted to say. But he remained silent, biting his tongue. What would have been the point? He had done it, done what she wanted, what was the point in spoiling it all now?

'Quite a performance,' she said. 'You're quite a man.'

She started to unstrap one of the ankle cuffs. He opened his eyes to watch but said nothing. Her back glistened with oil.

'You enjoy being tied down?'

'It's what you wanted.' He couldn't keep the annoyance out of his voice.

'I'm sorry, Jason,' she said unexpectedly, the first time he'd ever heard her use those words. Her expression was the one he had seen by the pool – a look of youth and innocence, so unlike what she had been only minutes before. He could see what she could have looked like as a young girl.

'Sorry for what?' There were so many things.

'For using you.'

'Using me like this?'

'No.' She changed her mind. 'Yes... I saw you sneaking in. There's an alarm on the other side of the drive too.'

'You could have called security.'

'I could have... I don't know why I did it. What's the matter with me, Jason?' The youthful face looked as though it were about to cry. 'I get sort of crazy...'

'It's all right...' He'd never seen her like this before.

'But it's not just this. I'd been thinking about it. I really fucked you around, Jason. I admit it. You were right...'

What had brought this on Jason didn't know. She

was stroking his leg very gently but made no attempt to unstrap the rest of the cuffs. If his arms had been free he would have cuddled her.

'I use men. I know I do. I guess it's a sort of payback for what they did to me, well what one did to me. I shouldn't have done it.'

'Look we all do things we regret.'

'Sure we do. So I'm trying to say sorry. I wish I could go back.'

'Back?'

'I'd like to make it up to you . . .'

'Really?' That was the best news Jason had heard for a long time.

'Trouble is I'm locked in now. *Casting Couch* is all set to roll. I've signed up the lead.'

'Who?'

'Al's playing the part.'

In a flash Jason suddenly realised where he'd seen Al before. He had been in Hanna's office at the studio when Jason had burst in on discovering they were auditioning for his part.

'And he's sleeping here?'

Hanna nodded.

'Oh . . .' The good news hadn't lasted long. Jason felt anger welling up inside him. He tried to sit up, momentarily forgetting the bonds and jerking against them. 'Let me up.'

Hanna moved to his wrist and was about to unbuckle the strap. 'Look, there's a good supporting part. You can play that. It's a good part really. I'll see you get a good deal . . .'

'For real this time?'

'For real. I promise you, Jason.' Hanna looked into

his eyes trying to show him how sincere she was.

She had made him promises before but this time he thought it was safe to believe her. It would be galling to see Al playing the lead but a good supporting part was better than nothing, and much better than another porno film.

'Don't let me down again,' he said quietly.

'I promise.'

She lent forward and kissed his lips very gently. He felt close to her, as if she had allowed him to see a part of her that she normally kept private. This time he thought she would keep her promise.

At that moment the bedroom door burst open.

'Hanna, darling, can I borrow your—'

A tall brunette had bounced into the room. She was wearing a black satin and lace suspender belt, sheer black stockings, a pair of tiny matching black panties smoothed tightly across her iron flat belly, and spiky high-heel shoes. Her breasts, plump proud melons of breasts, were naked.

Her jaw dropped as she took in the scene before her. She didn't retreat in embarrassment, but advanced right up to the bed, her eyes riveted to Jason's body.

'My god, Hanna, I didn't know you were into this . . .'

Of course, Jason recognised the woman immediately. It was Gloria Black, the winner of last year's Oscar for Best Actress.

'Look at this . . . he's come undone.'

Gloria was looking at the one ankle Hanna had unstrapped. She stooped, her heavy breasts hanging down between her arms, caught Jason's leg and before he'd realised what she was doing, had strapped it back into the leather cuff.

'What did you want, Gloria?' Hanna said calmly, seemingly unfazed by the intrusion.

Gloria laughed. 'Well, I wanted to borrow that white Valentino dress of yours. But now, well ... I'd like to borrow some of this. He's pretty isn't he?'

'Very,' Hanna agreed.

'Where's Al?'

'Having breakfast.'

'So can I have some breakfast too?' Gloria nodded toward Jason's body.

Looking up at Gloria's body – the black welts of the stockings pulled into chevrons on her creamy thighs by the taut suspenders, the satin of the panties covering the plane of her sex so smoothly the only crease where they had been dimpled by the furrow of her sex, her big mounds of breasts trembling every time she moved – was having an effect on Jason. He felt his cock stirring.

Hanna looked into his eyes. The look was a question. It was definitely a breakthrough in their relationship. A month ago, even, perhaps, an hour ago Hanna would not have bothered to ask. She would have simply let Gloria use him, an object of no account. Now she was giving him the chance to say no. It was a chance he had no intention of taking.

'Help yourself,' Hanna said getting up. She unhooked a towelling robe from the back of the bathroom door.

'You're full of surprises,' Gloria said.

'So is Jason ...' Hanna winked at him and walked to the bedroom door, closing it after her.

Slowly Gloria came round the bed. She hooked her thumbs into the waistband of the panties, deliberately turned her back on him, bent over and pulled the panties down. She had a fully meaty arse, the cleft between her buttocks dark and deep. As the panties reached her feet, Jason could see the whole furrow of her labia covered in short, black, very fine hair. As she turned, he saw the triangle of her belly, the short hairs all pointing in the same direction, pointing to the apex of her thighs.

She picked the panties off the floor.

'You've made me wet already,' she said dropping the panties on his face. They were damp and he could smell the scent of her sex. She knelt next to him on the bed. 'Now for my breakfast,' she said, her mouth lapping its way down his body to his cock, his erection growing stronger by the second ...

Chapter Six

It had been a long afternoon.

'Please don't. I can't take any more.'
'You have no choice.'
'It's my turn.'
'Get the whip on him if he won't do it.'

'OK, that's fine. On to the next.' The dubbing editor's voice came over the tannoy. Jason was sitting in a soundproof recording booth watching scenes from *Escape of the Whores* and 're-voicing' the parts of the dialogue that had been muffled or badly recorded.

The screen went blank, then exploded with light as Jason saw a close-up of his cock being shared out between three women, one of them holding it in her hand and offering it to the other two in turn. Another hand snaked up between his thighs and held his balls, juggling them with its fingers.

The picture cut to his face. Jason had had to employ all his talents to get the look of ecstasy that was required. In fact, his cock had felt raw and oversensitive after too much use.

'You're going to make me come,' he said, trying to match the words to the movement of his lips on the screen.

'Come on my face,' one of the girls said.

'Fine, just one more, Jason,' the disembodied voice from the control room said.

The screen went blank again, then sprang to life

with another scene. This time it was Camilla Potts laying on the bed, the camera lingering on her exquisite, naked body as she plunged a dildo into her sex, her legs spread wide open. Jason was being made to watch, his hands tied behind his back, two of the girls standing on either side of him holding him securely.

'Wouldn't you just love to be able to fuck me?' Camilla taunted.

'Yes, yes, for god's sake let me get at you,' Jason said into the microphone, trying to fill his voice with frustration.

'Again,' the editor commanded.

The film wound backward, then forward again. Jason repeated the line.

'OK. Done. That's a wrap.'

The lights went up and the studio door opened, the editor beaming a smile at Jason.

'Great film. I think it's going to be bigger than *Deep Throat*.'

Jason hoped desperately that it wouldn't, in fact he hoped it would be buried forever and never seen again.

'Can I go?'

'Sure, we're all done here.'

Pulling on his leather jacket, Jason looked at his watch. He'd told Nancy he'd be back by six and it was seven already. She was cooking for them tonight.

Having learnt from experience that there were no taxis cruising the streets of LA, he got the studio to call him a cab while he rang Nancy to tell her he was going to be late.

'Hello,' the voice on the phone sounded husky and out of breath.

'Nancy?' He wasn't at all sure it was her.
'Jason...'
'Look I'm going to be late. I'm leaving now.'
'Fine... oh that's... that's fine...'
'Are you all right?'
'Oh yes... yes... yes...'
The dialling tone replaced the voice.

Thirty minutes later, still wondering why Nancy had been so abrupt, the taxi dropped Jason off outside Nancy's small house. He walked around the back, through the garden, expecting to see Nancy in the kitchen through the big patio window. But there was no sign of her, and no sign of discarded cooking either. She had certainly not started to prepare a meal.

Puzzled, Jason let himself in through the back door and went inside. The house appeared empty. There was a bottle of wine open on the kitchen counter, which had not been there when he left at lunch time, but no sign of Nancy.

It was not until he wandered into the hall that he heard the noise. It was a soft gasp, barely audible, an exhalation of air, a sigh of pleasure. The bedroom door was ajar.

Quietly Jason tiptoed along the hall to the door, looking in through the crack by the hinges, just as he heard another plaintive cry.

He recognised the beautiful apple-shaped bottom that he could see sticking up on the bed. He had seen it most of the afternoon on film. It belonged to Camilla Potts. Between her thighs, her mouth pressed hard against Camilla's sex, was Nancy's head, her long hair streaming over the white sheet. Camilla, in turn, had her face buried between Nancy's legs, her arms wrapped around her thighs holding them up in the air at right angles to her body.

The two women moaned periodically as one or the other's tongue probed a particularly sensitive nerve, and provoked an instinctive involuntary reaction.

'So this is what you were up to?' Jason said walking into the room.

Neither woman paid the slightest bit of notice. He could see Nancy's mouth sucking on Camilla's hairless labia, a regular, relentless rhythm. He stood by the bed and caressed the long curve of Camilla's spine, then moved his hand to Nancy's outstretched leg. He saw Camilla's head bobbing up and down on Nancy's sex, the two women's movements synchronised, too near to orgasm to do anything but continue.

He watched, fascinated, as Camilla's slender body, her knees bent up under her torso, responded to Nancy's mouth. He could see it tightening, her whole body imitating the rhythm of her sex, straining for its release. Exactly the same thing was happening to Nancy. Both women were poised, their bodies locked together so perfectly, so tightly that they felt everything the other was feeling, like a doubling of their own sensation, their own excitement added to by the impossibility of ignoring the other's pleasure. Each stroke of the tongue, each little nudge against the clitoris, each probe into the mouth of their sex, was magnified by the fact that they felt the response and the stimulus at exactly the same moment, like sound trapped in a valley, echoing back and forth.

Finally, it was too much.

'Please, please . . .' Nancy gasped into Camilla's sex as her body gave up the struggle to remain in control.

RETURN TO THE CASTING COUCH

At exactly the same time, she felt Camilla exhale against her and their bodies trembled violently as the double orgasm shook through them, the reverberations in Camilla affecting Nancy and vice versa.

It went on for a long time too, unwilling to let them go, not the first orgasm they had shared that afternoon, but certainly the best, perhaps enhanced by knowing they were being watched.

'Darling...' Nancy said as Camilla rolled off her. 'At least you didn't miss the main feature...' She smiled, her face still slack, like someone who'd had too much to drink, her mouth wet with Camilla's juices.

'I wondered what you were doing on the phone.'

'I got your message on my answerphone...' Camilla said. 'As I was passing I thought I'd drop in...'

'And she decided to wait,' Nancy added with a wicked smile. It was not the first time since they had been together that Nancy had taken the opportunity to do to Camilla what she had seen her do so many times on video.

'So I see.'

'I'm glad I did. All this sucking is good but it makes me hot for cock,' Camilla said.

'Mmm... me too.' Nancy wiped her mouth dry with her fingers. 'And Jason's been watching you on screen all afternoon.'

'Have you?'

'Dubbing,' he explained.

'Well, you must be randy then. How was I?'

'Very steamy. The editor thinks it'll be bigger than *Deep Throat*.'

'You're going to have the most famous cock in the country,' Nancy said.

'Don't joke.'

'Who's joking? Come on, Jason. Don't keep me waiting. Enough talk . . .' Nancy reached out to the fly of Jason's jeans and pulled the zip down. As she unbuckled his belt and pulled the jeans down around his hips Camilla slid off the bed.

'You got any stockings?' she asked Nancy. 'I feel like getting dressed up.'

'Second drawer in the dresser. Help yourself.'

'I love dressing up . . .' Camilla said going over to the dressing table and opening Nancy's lingerie drawer. She explored it for a while, going through the panties and silky nylons before extracting a pair of white stockings and a lacy white basque.

'This is good. Nice and tight.'

Camilla fished in the drawer again, found a pair of black stockings and a wide black suspender belt and came back to the bed, dropping all the lingerie on the sheet. Cooperating with Nancy, Camilla stripped the rest of Jason's clothes off. His cock sprang up from his boxer shorts as they were pulled off last of all. Nancy kissed it briefly.

'There's a good boy,' she said, looking right at it.

'Sit and watch now,' Camilla said sternly.

Jason climbed on to the bed, put two pillows behind his back and did exactly as he was told. Even as little as six months ago he might have imagined being in bed with two long-legged full-breasted brunettes, of them pandering to him and to each other, but he would never have dreamt that it would become a reality, let alone that he would be living with a woman who seemed to want to take every opportunity to indulge her very liberal sexual tastes, a woman who would not only get a thrill from hearing of his escapades with other women, but would be only too delighted to use them as part of her own pleasure. Nancy was a very extraordinary woman. And so, of course, was Camilla.

Camilla picked up one of the black stockings. She rolled it into a pocket and indicated to Nancy that she should extend her leg. Nancy pointed her foot and let Camilla play the stocking out over her creamy flesh, repeating the process with the other one. As soon as the stockings were in place, Camilla took the lacy suspender belt, wrapped it around Nancy's waist and clipped it on. Taking each suspender in turn, she pulled the welt of the stocking taut, slipped the little nub of rubber under the nylon, then pressed it into the metal hoop, trapping the stocking top.

She saw Jason's eyes following her fingers, watching all the planes and angles and shades and shadows the lingerie created, moulding and shaping the body, the expanse of naked thigh above the stocking top seemingly impossibly soft and creamy in contrast to the shiny web of black nylon.

Camilla stood up. Jason could never quite get over the spectacle of Camilla's tits. Big and very round they seemed to defy gravity. Their summit, topped by her hard nipples, actually tilted upward. He loved the way they pressed against each other, forming a natural cleavage, as deep and dark as the one that separated her buttocks.

Camilla rolled one of the white stockings into a pocket as she had done with the black. Then she put her foot on the bed, her naked body turned towards Jason so he could see the triangle of her belly, hairless and exposed, and her labia beneath, reddened and swollen by their recent activity. She inserted her foot in the pocket of white and very slowly drew it up over her long leg, looking up to see Jason's eyes on her hands as they played the material out over her tanned flesh, the nylon making a rasping whispering noise as she pulled it taut. Satisfied it was smooth, she replaced one foot with the other allowing Jason to see how this made her labia move, the two lips rubbing against each other.

With the two stockings in place, she picked up the white basque and wrapped it around her body.

'Do me up,' she said to Nancy. 'Tight.'

The low-cut bra of the basque fitted Camilla's breasts surprisingly well, Nancy's tits being more pendulous but about the same size. Nancy's body was bigger overall, however, and she had to use the tightest row of outer hooks to cinch the girdle around Camilla's slimmer waist. It did not take long for the suspenders, hanging down from the bottom of the basque to be hooked into the white welts of the stockings. Camilla took her time, adjusting the stockings until they were held firmly in place, the nylon smooth and unwrinkled.

'Well now,' she said, taking Nancy's hand and getting her to stand beside her. She turned her so they were facing each other, then moved her body forward until her lace-covered breasts just grazed Nancy's bare rigid nipples. She brushed them by swaying her body from side to side, then bent to flick each nipple with her tongue.

They turned to look at Jason. He had taken his cock in his hand and was wanking it slowly. The sight and sound of the two women dressing so erotically, their bodies now the picture of sensuality, the sheer stockings making their slender legs shimmer, the contrast between the two of them – Nancy's mat of pubic hair in comparison to Camilla's total lack – as lickerish as the similarities – their long legs and heavy breasts. Jason's cock was ready.

As Camilla appeared to know exactly what she wanted, Nancy followed her lead. Camilla knelt on the bed alongside Jason's hips. Nancy walked around the bed to kneel on the other side of him. Camilla indicated that he should slide down the bed and he obeyed, looking into her eyes and being thrilled by what he saw there. She dipped her head and sucked the head of his cock into her mouth. Nancy leant forward to suck on the lower end of his shaft.

'God...' he gasped as their mouths went to work, tonguing and lapping and sucking his cock, the two brunette heads bobbing in his lap – Camilla's short beautifully cut bob shaking as she moved, Nancy's long flowing hair streaming out on his thighs. 'You're going to make me come,' he warned. He had said that already today.

'No, we're not,' Camilla said, the words muffled on his cock.

She twisted herself round, swung a leg over Jason's chest and sunk her mouth deeper on to his hard phallus. This had the effect of pushing Nancy further down, her mouth settling on his balls. She sucked them in eagerly.

Jason looked up Camilla's long contoured thighs. If her tits were extraordinary so was this view of her sex – poised above his face, the supple round cushions of her buttocks neatly bisected by the deep furrow that ran between them, every crease and fold and wrinkle exposed by the absence of hair, the ring of her anus striated as regularly as a clock face, and below it the labia, hairless and smooth, its thick rubbery flesh glistening with the wetness her previous orgasms had produced. Her sex was like a rare orchid, the pinks and reds of the outer lips giving way to the crimson and scarlet of the centre, the mouth open, its interior the darkest red of them all.

Over the last few months, Jason had looked at Camilla's naked sex many times – in this room with Nancy, on the film set surrounded by people – but he would never forget the first time he'd seen it, what seemed like a lifetime ago now. She had been standing naked in a bathroom at the Dorchester Hotel in London and he'd blundered in by mistake. The room's mirrored walls reflected every angle, every nuance, every curve of her perfect figure and the look in her eyes had been every bit as exciting as the one he had seen a few seconds ago.

The memory made his cock surge.

'Mmm . . .' Camilla responded feeling him swell, wriggling her bum and lowering it further until her labia were inches from his mouth.

Jason needed no further encouragement. Wrapping his arms around her thighs, he levered himself up and stuck his tongue, as deep as it would go, into the crimson mouth of her sex, rolling it around inside. He tasted her juices, as he had so many times before, and smelt the musky aroma of sex. Moving his mouth further up her sleek labia, he reached for her clitoris, another familiar landmark on the map of her body. He felt her mouth tense on his cock as his tongue tapped against it. At that moment he felt Nancy release his balls, allowing them to slip gently out of her mouth. She was moving around but he could not see what she was doing, the glorious prospect of Camilla's buttocks and thighs blocking his view.

Camilla sat up, altering the angle of her sex against Jason's mouth, sitting on his face, pushing his head back on the bed but not putting him off the tempo he had established on her clit.

Nancy faced Camilla, knelt over Jason's hips and, using her hand as a guide, brought the head of his cock to the lips of her cunt. The two women kissed, hard and deeply, their tongues in and out of each other's mouths, their breasts crushed together, Nancy holding herself over Jason's cock but not on it, not yet. She broke the kiss. Looking down at Camilla's body, crammed into the tight white basque, her thighs bisected by the white welts of the stockings, the suspenders slack, looped out by her position, Nancy folded the lacy bra cups of the basque down under her breasts, one after the other. Then, with the fingers of both hands she pinched her nipples, lifting her breasts up by them so they were stretched towards her throat.

Jason could not see what she was doing but felt its effect. As his tongue beat out a relentless tattoo on the little nut of her clitoris, he felt her labia contract and a flood of juices flow from her sex, almost as though she had spunked, the sap of her body flowing over his chin. She was on the brink, he knew.

He tried to concentrate, tried to ignore his cock, the feeling of Nancy's hairy labia against his glans, formed like a kiss, making him want to plunge it home. He hammered against Camilla's clit harder, holding her down on his face with his hands wrapped around her thighs, feeling the nylon of the stockings where it gave way to naked flesh under his palms.

Nancy did not let go of her nipples. The pain from them – level, steady, aching pain that turned to waves of sexual heat – and the constant rapping of Jason's tongue was irresistible. Camilla looked at Nancy's body, Jason's big cock held between her thighs, the profuse growth of black pubic curls on her belly framed by the black stockings and suspenders she had drawn up her silky legs, her large ovoid breasts hanging down from her chest, mounds of spongy, pliant flesh quivering with excitement. Then she looked into her eyes and saw how they were watching her, wanting and needing, she knew, to see her come.

And Nancy would get her wish. Camilla told her, used her eyes to tell her she was coming, to show her how her body had passed the point of no return and was falling now, cascading down into total sensation. As long as she could, she held her eyes open wanting Nancy to see them, her eyes the window to the soul of her orgasm. But then it was too much and they rolled back, the whites replacing the pupils, her orgasm sending pleasure to the nerves behind them, stinging them with feeling as Camilla's body shook violently, as if seized by a giant hand and tossed to and fro.

Nancy released her breasts and sank down on to the hard shaft of Jason's cock, wriggling her hips to impale herself on it. She loved this, all of it. Ever since Jason had walked into her life, closely followed by the beautiful Camilla, it had been transformed, at least her sex life had. Of course, she had had many lovers, and some of them had been good, but it was never enough for her. She was hungry, her body never satisfied, always wanting more. She'd started collecting movies, porno movies, and lay in bed at night, watching scenes of wild debauchery, while she played with herself, dildoes crammed into both passages of her body, and one in her mouth, while her fingers strummed her clitoris like the strings of a guitar.

Now the scenes were real and even included some of the cast. Now she could touch and kiss and wank and suck Camilla Potts as she'd seen her being touched and kissed and wanked and sucked so many times on screen. Now she would do anything, satisfy her hunger and longing, eat at the table of lust until she was replete.

As she watched Camilla's body slacken, the orgasm slowly releasing its hold on her, she felt the hardness of Jason's cock buried inside her. Pulling herself off him, until he was all but out of her, she fell on him again, feeling him stabbing into her. She started a rhythm, bouncing up and down on his rock-hard erection.

Camilla took one of her breasts in her hand. It was too big for her to contain all of it in her fingers and the spongy flesh escaped on all sides like lumps of dough. Her other hand caressed Nancy's belly, her forefinger searching through the forest of hair until it lighted on Nancy's clitoris. The tip of her finger skated across it, pushing it hard into the pubic bone, before moving it gently up and down, using the same tempo Nancy used to slide up and down on Jason's cock.

'Oh, that's good . . .' Nancy said.

It was Camilla's turn to watch, watch Nancy's body tense, watch that incredible look in her eyes as they stared back at her, the look that changed from interest, from admiration and appreciation of beauty, to desire, from desire to need and from need to fulfilment, as sensation exploded in her soft brown pupils like fireworks against the night sky and her body trembled as Jason's cock and Camilla's hands wrung her orgasm out of her, and her eyes were finally closed by her passion.

Slowly Camilla let go of her breasts and watched as the orgasm ran its course, Nancy's body changing from rigidity to relaxation as she came down from her high. Camilla climbed off the bed. Nancy did the same. They looked down at Jason. His face was wet with Camilla's spending, his cock and thighs from Nancy's. His phallus stuck up from his body at right angles, red and angry-looking, its need only too obvious.

'Such a difficult choice, isn't it, big boy?' Nancy said, her hand circling his cock and squeezing it hard. 'Who do you want to spunk?'

He had an answer for that. It was his turn now and he knew exactly what he wanted to do.

'Turn round . . . on all fours,' he said to Camilla as he got to his knees on the bed.

'My lucky night, is it?' she said.

'You too,' Jason told Nancy. 'On all fours, side by side.'

They both looked puzzled but did as they were told. The two women knelt on the bed side by side, Nancy to the left, Camilla on the right. They faced the foot of the bed, their hips touching, their legs apart, their buttocks thrust up into the air, the slits of their sex exposed – one bare, sleek and smooth, the other matted with black hair – both their thighs bisected by the welts of their stockings – black on one, white on the other.

RETURN TO THE CASTING COUCH

Camilla's slender back was clad in tight elasticated silky nylon, Nancy's divided by the wide strip of the black lace suspender belt. Two women, eager, expectant, compliant, their sexes so wet, a slick of dampness was visible in the hollows at the top of their thighs.

Which to choose? He wasn't going to choose. Crawling forward on his knees he got between Nancy's legs, guiding his cock into her labia. He used his right hand to caress Camilla's buttocks, then slipped it down on to her sex. Simultaneously, he drove his cock into Nancy and his fingers, three fingers into Camilla. Both women gasped with pleasure. With no subtlety and no gentleness, he drove both as deep as they would go. Then he began a rhythm, pulling both back and forth at the same time, the action of one imitating the action of the other.

It was not going to take him long to come, not after everything he'd seen and done, not after watching Camilla pull the stockings on to Nancy's legs and then her own, not having tongued Camilla's sex and felt her orgasm and Nancy's shaking through their bodies.

He pumped back and forth then withdrew, cock and hand. Quickly he jumped over their legs, positioned his cock behind Camilla and his hand behind Nancy and drove the two forward again. A few more strokes with both and he moved again, from one to the other, replacing his fingers with his cock and vice versa.

Their cunts felt different – Nancy's looser and bigger but seeming to suck him in more like a mouth; Camilla's tighter, clinging to him more, harder to penetrate. He pumped Nancy with his cock while his fingers reamed into Camilla's again. Both women were excited by the experience. They were making little mewing noises, almost inaudible; occasionally he could see them looking at each other, and moving their lips to kiss, though only briefly.

He was coming, coming in Nancy's cunt. He felt his spunk pumping up into his shaft. This was going to be hard, needed all his control. He gritted his teeth, his face forming a grim rictus of concentration.

In seconds he felt his cock begin to jerk and spit spunk into the silky walls of Nancy's sex. Instantly, and against all his instincts, he pulled his spurting cock out of her body, heaved himself over to Camilla and plugged his cock into her, plunging it deep then letting himself go, letting his spunk jet out in its final resting place in Camilla's liquid centre.

It seemed to last forever, the unwarranted interruption fuelling the final spasms.

He looked down at them. Spunk had lashed over both their buttocks as he transferred from one to the other.

'That was quite a trick,' Camilla said looking over her shoulder at him.

'Two for the price of one,' he said before collapsing back on to the wrinkled sheets.

It was a balmy night, the best time of the day, a pleasantly warm breeze blowing in from the sea.

They sat on the patio in Nancy's lush garden, the heavy scent of many flowers hanging in the air, a carafe of Californian wine on the table in front of them, the remnants of bread and cheese and sliced salami on the table too, Nancy having decided she was too tired to cook.

Camilla had borrowed a pair of Nancy's black Lycra leggings and a leotard, the smart suit she had arrived in hanging in the bedroom, while Nancy was comfortable in a tracksuit and Jason wore his usual T-shirt and jeans. They were relaxed together, all their appetites satisfied.

'So what did you call me about?' Camilla asked. She had got Jason's message on her answerphone, but he'd only left his number.

'Well, I just thought we should all get together.'

'It was my idea,' Nancy said. 'I wanted a rerun...'

'But I've got news too,' Jason added. 'Did Nancy tell you about Harriet Teitelbaum?'

'No, she was too busy seducing me...'

'You didn't take much persuading,' Nancy said.

'Of course not. With a body like yours you should be in the movies.' Camilla touched Nancy's hand.

'You think so?'

'Sure. And you'd enjoy it wouldn't you?'

'I might.' She was trying to imagine what it would be like.

'So what about Harriet?' Camilla asked.

'I took a script round.'

'You got in to see her?' Camilla sounded surprised.

'Not exactly.'

Jason told her what had happened, not omitting any of the details of his encounter with Cynthia.

'Sounds promising,' Camilla said when he'd finished.

'Depending on how you see Cynthia's role in the domestic arrangements.' Nancy said. Jason had told her his doubts about Cynthia's promises.

'You never can tell,' Camilla added. 'Still it's better than nothing.'

'And he's back in with Hanna Silverstein,' Nancy told her.

'Really and how did you do that?'

'To tell you the truth I'm not entirely sure. She just seemed to change, go all soft, then she apologised... actually said she was sorry for the way she'd treated me.'

'Hard to credit.'

'Exactly. I've still no idea what brought it on...'

'Tell Auntie Camilla all. What did you do precisely? Knowing Hanna, it must have had something to do with sex.'

'You guessed.'

Jason went through all the details, describing what he had been made to do with Al. He decided to omit the episode with Gloria Black.

'Interesting,' Camilla said, sipping her wine.

'So I'm back in *The Casting Couch*.'

'That's good.'

'But only in a supporting part. Not the lead. She's cast the lead.'

'Oh...' Camilla looked depressed but then smiled. 'Still it's better than nothing.'

'It's better than...' He was just about to say 'another porno film' but stopped himself. 'It's better than being out of work,' he re-phrased quickly, bearing in mind Camilla's occupation.

'Sure. And if Cynthia comes good...'

'Then we'll have a party.' Jason said.

'Just the three of us,' Nancy added sliding her foot up under the table and resting it on Jason's thigh.

'I'll drink to that,' Camilla said, sliding her foot up to rest on Nancy's lap.

They each sipped at their wine and listened to the cicadas, their constant chirping sound as much a part of life in LA as the smog. It was late by now but Camilla appeared in no hurry to go home...

Chapter Seven

The car arrived at five minutes to eight. It was due at eight. The driver – a tall negress, her hair cropped to within an inch of her head, the black suit she wore revealing most of her long, elegant legs clad in shiny sheer hosiery – sat behind the wheel, waiting for the five minutes to pass. She left the engine of the ultra-stretch white Cadillac running so its air conditioner could keep the big interior cool and its refrigerator, set into a panel behind the driver's partition, maintained the chill on the champagne and ice it was stacked in.

The printed invitation had arrived in the post after a very formal call from a secretary to establish Jason's address. It was printed on stiff white card, rimmed in gold, and requested the pleasure of his company – and his guest – at a reception to be held in the J. Paul Getty Museum, Pacific Coast Highway, Malibu, to celebrate the presentation to the museum of a gift by Ms Harriet Teitelbaum. Jason imagined the secretary had been given the telephone number by Cynthia – he'd scrawled it on the script as he'd left the penthouse. But by whatever means the invitation had arrived, it seemed to represent a very positive step in the right direction.

If Harriet Teitelbaum had hated the script, or had not even bothered to read it, she was hardly likely to invite Jason and guest to a party out of the blue. It appeared, at the very least, he *had* underestimated

Cynthia. It was not a mistake he would make again.

Ringing to accept on the number printed at the bottom of the card alongside RSVP, Jason had been told a car would be sent to pick him up – an added luxury which Nancy, who knew more of the foibles of Hollywood, assured him meant he was on the VIP guest list.

Nancy, who had squeezed her hips into a strapless figure-hugging dark blue dress – which showed off her ample cleavage and the spectacular curvature of her buttocks, and which she had bought specially for the occasion – was particularly impressed when the Cadillac had pulled up outside.

'That's the double stretch,' she told him. 'That's a very good sign.'

'How good?'

'I'd say she's-read-the-script good.'

Nancy slipped into her black high heels and finished pinning her hair up so her long neck would compliment her bare shoulders. She applied a coat of lipstick to her very full lips and stood waiting for his opinion.

'Will I do?'

'Just great.'

'And you.'

He was wearing an Armani suit he'd brought with the proceeds from *Escape of the Whores*, and a tieless silk shirt.

'You look good enough to eat,' he said, caressing her silk-covered bottom.

'I hope that's a promise,' she said as the doorbell rang.

'Your carriage awaits, madam,' he said.

'How very English . . .'

RETURN TO THE CASTING COUCH

Jason opened the front door.

'Car for Mr MacIver,' the black chauffeuse said, eyeing Jason appreciatively.

'We're ready,' he said, escorting Nancy to the car after locking the front door. The chauffeuse opened the huge rear passenger door, nearly twice the width of a normal door.

'There's champagne in the fridge, sir, and all the usual drinks in the cocktail cabinet,' she said as Jason got in.

The interior was vast. A wool rug, so thick it swallowed most of their shoes, carpeted the floor, while a black leather bench seat across the back cossetted them in the depths of comfort. The care had every conceivable accessory. Besides the cocktail cabinet and fridge the chauffeuse had mentioned, each side of the car had its own telephone mounted within easy range of each passenger's hand. There was a control panel on either side too, with controls for the radio, television, video recorder, air conditioning, electrically adjustable seats and all the windows, including the driver's partition.

'She says there's champagne,' Jason told Nancy.

'I heard.'

'Shall we?'

'Oh definitely, I think.'

He opened the fridge door and extracted the bottle and two glasses, setting them down in a round wooden receptacle designed to hold them steady while he opened the bottle and the chauffeuse pulled the car out into traffic. There was a receptacle for the bottle too which he used as soon as he'd filled the glasses. He handed one to Nancy.

'The champagne treatment,' he said.

'It bodes well Jason . . . I think this is going to be fun.'

'I just hope she's read the script.'

They lapsed into silence, sitting back in the comfort of the leather seats, watching the world go by through the tinted windows of the limousine, sipping the champagne, the soft suspension of the car having a soporific effect, all of which added to Jason's feeling that tonight might well be a night to remember. His eyes drifted to Nancy's crossed legs. The skirt of the dress had ridden up on her thighs and her long powerful-looking limbs shimmered in their fine nylon tights.

The journey out to Malibu did not take long. They had only gone through half the champagne when the chauffeuse guided the car into the driveway of the museum. They were on a hill overlooking the ocean, its neatly planted gardens dotted with impressive sculptures among which Jason recognised a monumental Henry Moore and two of the most famous Rodins.

The drive was lined with expensive motor cars – Ferraris, every colour and model of Mercedes, three or four convertible Jaguars and Rolls Royces. Car jockeys in peach-coloured jackets ran to and fro between them and the entrance as more guests arrived to be valet-parked.

The white Cadillac halted and the black chauffeuse opened the rear passenger door on Nancy's side. They climbed out.

'Have a nice evening,' she said politely.

'Thank you.'

RETURN TO THE CASTING COUCH

The area in front of the main museum doors had been roped off and perhaps a hundred people pressed in from both sides, eager to see 'stars' arrive. There had been a rustle of excitement as their big stretch pulled up but it soon dissipated as Nancy and Jason were dismissed as 'nobodies'. One day, Jason thought cheerfully, perhaps they won't be so unimpressed. He was more and more convinced that the omens for him and the Len Furey script looked good.

They walked through into the airy light and extremely well-designed museum. Waitresses, modestly dressed by Hollywood standards in gold leotards and matching ra-ra skirts, like football-team cheerleaders, circulated with trays of champagne, water, orange juice or red wine. To one side there was a bar with every possible spirit for the more serious drinkers, though most people drank only mineral water.

Around the walls, well protected from the party people by perspex screens, Jason could see the numerous masterpieces the Getty wealth had bought for the people of Los Angeles: Picassos, Braques, Rembrandts, Van Goghs and Gauguins, to say nothing of Titian and Goya and de Vinci. There appeared to be no theme to the collection, no one period collected above another, the only rationale that the paintings had all been bought for the highest prices.

Taking champagne from a passing waitress Jason and Nancy mingled among the guests. The prices of the star actors who stood around the room chatting, mostly to each other, were in the same class as the prices paid for the pictures. It seemed every top star was here, the men dressed in everything from T-shirt and jeans to elegant tuxedos, the women just as diverse except that all, without exception, wore various creations from the haute couture houses of Beverly Hills, or from their own private couturier.

There were not only movies stars. There were political high-rollers too – the Governor of California and several senators Jason recognised from news interviews. There were two English painters who had both made their homes in the city and an American rock band.

Nancy had nodded and smiled at several of the guests but as yet had seen no one she knew well.

'This is very in,' she whispered. 'Big money.'

'Can you see Cyn or Harry?'

'They must be here somewhere.'

Down the centre of the room, a huge rectangular table had been set up, with two vast circular flower displays of white lillies and orchids at each end, and an enormous swan carved from ice in the centre. Between them was an array of every sort of food: lobsters, langoustine, oysters, clams, *foie gras*, caviar, numerous exotic salads, bowls of fruit and moulded Bavarian creams, as well as cakes and pastries in every shade and colour.

It was at the end of the table with all the desserts that Jason finally spotted Cynthia, standing alone, forking mouthfuls of chocolate cake into her mouth so hastily that there was a brown stain around her lips. Nudging Nancy to indicate their quarry, Jason took her hand and lead her over to the table.

'Jason, hi,' Cynthia said enthusiastically as soon as she saw him ploughing through the crowd. Cynthia looked like a model from a Paris catwalk, dressed by one of the more outré designers. Her feet were tied into big platform-soled heels by a criss-cross of white satin ribbon. The same ribbon had been used to construct a dress that looked as though her body had been wrapped by a rather bad embalmer from ancient Egypt, covering some parts and not others, revealing strips of naked flesh on her buttocks and navel with one whole breast exposed and ribbon barely covering the other. Over this she wore a full-length robe made from white silk thread, fashioned to resemble a spider's web, its centre positioned over Cynthia's small naked breast.

'Hi, Cyn,' Jason said.

Cynthia kissed him on both cheeks, transferring chocolate and lipstick to his face.

'This is Nancy.'

'Pleased to meet you, Nancy. So you're the lucky girl.'

'For the time being,' Nancy had taken a tiny white handkerchief from her evening bag and was dabbing it on Jason's cheeks to remove the marks.

'Sorry, did I do that? Gee, I can't leave chocolate alone. I'd like to bathe in the stuff.'

'Here,' Nancy offered her the handkerchief and a little mirror from her bag.

'Thanks,' she removed the stains, wetting the material with her tongue. 'Great party.'

'Harry must have a lot of friends.'

'Harry's powerful. In Hollywood that means you have a lot of friends,' she said with surprising realism.

'Where is she?' Jason asked.

'Up there talking to the museum big wigs.' Cynthia indicated a gallery high above the main room. Four men and two women stood in conversation, except that one of the 'men' was in fact Harriet Teitelbaum, her pinstriped suit, shirt and tie every bit as well-tailored as the others. 'She's going to like you,' Cyn added, looking at Nancy.

Jason saw Harriet's attention was wandering; whatever the little man who was talking at her so intently was saying, it was obviously not making much of an impact on her. She looked down at the party below, searching among the familiar faces until her eyes lighted on Cynthia. They moved to Jason who smiled a greeting. Harriet smiled back, an odd thin smile. Jason saw her take her leave of the others and head down the stairs. After a few minutes, delayed by the fact that everyone who found Harriet at their elbows wanted to shake her hand – and, in the case of a few very brave souls, venture a kiss – she arrived at Cynthia's side.

'Glad you could make it,' she said to Jason, extending her hand to be shaken.

'Harry, this is Nancy...' Cynthia said, stumbling when she realised she didn't know Nancy's surname.

'Nancy Dockery,' Nancy said.

'How lovely, how lovely you look,' Harriet said taking Nancy by the bare shoulders and kissing her on both cheeks, her eyes dropping to Nancy's impressive cleavage. 'You look ravishing in that dress, my dear.'

'Thank you,' Nancy said a little overwhelmed by Harriet's obvious interest.

'Stunning,' Harriet added, her eyes still roaming Nancy's bosom as if trying to imagine what it looked like unfettered.

Faced with Harriet Teitelbaum in person, Jason was

unsure what to say. He wanted to ask about the script but thought perhaps he should wait until Harriet or Cynthia brought it up first.

'I've bought them a Rubens,' Harriet said.

'Really?'

'A Goya last year and a Rubens this. Not bad going. They wanted me to go on the board. Four and a half million dollars to get on the board!'

Harriet's appearance was so masculine – her hair parted and combed like a man, the shirt giving little hint of breasts, even her shoes highly polished male brogues – it was difficult to think of her as a woman. Her face had a slight oriental slant to it, her cheeks were rather chubby with a small nose. Made up, with a different hair cut, it could have been a feminine face, even a pretty one, but as it was, with the only hint of make-up a slight darkening of her eyebrows, the vaguest colouring on her cheeks, it did not appear out of place in its masculine setting. Only Harriet's voice betrayed her, light and feminine and even a little squeaky.

'I think I owe you an apology,' Harriet said, wrestling her eyes from Nancy at last and turning to Jason.

'Do you?'

'It was just that I didn't recognise the name when you came to my office . . .'

'Oh yes . . .'

'You must have thought me very rude. I hope you will forgive me?'

She sounded perfectly genuine, as though it were a matter of real concern.

'It's all right . . .'

'No, no, it isn't. That's why I wanted you *both*' – she stressed the word 'both' looking at Nancy again – 'to come tonight. I'd hate you to think I was the sort of person who ignores their friends.'

'Of course not.' The truth was Jason didn't know what to think. This display of politeness was as unexpected as the original invitation.

'Tell him about the film,' Cynthia said. Jason felt his heart leap. This was it.

'Yes, your script—'

'Harriet!'

A short but extremely burly man had come up behind Jason and was extending an arm around Harriet to give her an affectionate hug. Jason recognised him immediately. Wolfgang Wolf was probably Hollywood's hottest star, his action adventure movies grossing huge profits, companies queueing up to pay him the millions of dollars he demanded for displaying his muscles, overdeveloped from his years as a champion body-builder.

'Wolf...'

'Great party. Peter says you're going to do my next picture.'

'I can't afford you.'

'We'll do a deal. Come over and talk to him.'

'You're too expensive.'

'For you Harriet, I'll take half.'

'Put it in writing and you've got a deal.'

'I want to do the film. Come over and talk to him.'

'Sure.' Harriet half-turned then looked back at Jason. 'Just excuse me a second, Wolf. I'll be right there.'

Wolf smiled and walked away.

'Can't talk now...' Harriet said. 'I think I've just saved myself two million dollars. Are you doing anything this weekend? Both of you?'

'No,' Jason tried to hide the disappointment in his voice.

'Good. I'll have my car pick you up at six on Friday. Come and spend the weekend in the desert with me. I've got a delightful little place out there. Cyn would like it too, wouldn't you?'

'Great.'

'All settled then.'

'Did you read the script?' Jason asked, desperate for some morsel of encouragement.

'Sure, sure... we'll talk on Friday.' And with that Harriet hustled Cynthia away to where Wolfgang Wolf was talking to a tall, prematurely white-haired man, though his body language was still angled towards Harriet. Jason watched as he greeted her again, a huge smile on his face.

'Well, that's that,' he said to Nancy, the wake that Harriet and Cynthia had cut through the crowd gradually filling up and hiding them from sight.

'It's definitely not a no, is it?'

'It's definitely not a yes either,' Jason said.

'It's a definite maybe,' Nancy added, smiling at one of the oldest jokes in Hollywood.

'So what do we do now?'

'How about we enjoy ourselves?'

'Hi!' The voice came from behind. Jason felt a hand goose his bottom hard. He turned to see Cheryl from Harriet's office.

'Hello,' Jason said, turning around. Cheryl was wearing the tightest hot pants he had ever seen, so tight the material cut into the furrow of her sex and the tops of her thighs. Above the pants she wore a cropped top in the same bright red, leaving her midriff bare. 'Cheryl, meet Nancy.'

Thankfully his encounter with Cheryl – and the services he had performed in the back of her old Buick convertible parked on Mulholland Drive in return for Harriet's address – had been reported to Nancy in detail.

'So you're the lucky one, are you?' Cheryl said, like an echo.

'Apparently so,' replied Nancy, without the slightest hint of jealousy. 'And you're the one with the convertible. I've always wanted a convertible.'

'And I've always wanted an Englishman. Doesn't that accent just drive you wild? Any time you want me to party you know the number, lover boy,' she said brightly before sashaying away through the crowd, the hot pants cutting into her buttocks so deeply that walking must have been painful.

Jason grabbed some more champagne from a passing golden girl and they roamed the room, talking to a lot of people, some of them stars. They ate the delicious food and danced together in a marquee that had been erected on the lawn, to a band who varied the music from rock to ballads. At one point in the evening there was a presentation, Harriet Teitelbaum formally handing over the Rubens to the Museum, while they, in turn, unveiled a little plaque that had been erected in her honour.

As people started drifting away Jason decided they should go too. Harriet and Cynthia were constantly surrounded by the rich and famous and Jason saw no point in trying to talk to them again.

They headed for the exit. In that mysterious way that good chauffeurs have, the white Cadillac was pulling up at the entrance seconds before they asked for it, still surrounded by hopeful fans. The black chauffeuse ran around to open the passenger door. As Nancy climbed in first, Jason looked into the driver's almost black eyes.

'I hope you had a good evening, sir,' she said.

'Yes, thank you,' he said, feeling his cock stir. There was something about the way she was looking at him. The moment passed and he got into the car, the chauffeuse closing the door after him.

As she got behind the wheel, she wound down the glass partition that divided her from the passengers.

'Where to sir, madam?'

Jason could see her eyes in the rear-view mirror. The look was far from cool disinterest.

'Where do you suggest?' he said, nudging Nancy to look in the mirror too.

'I meant, do you want to go straight home, or would you prefer the scenic route?'

'The scenic route would be nice.'

Almost before he'd finished the sentence the glass partition began to wind up with the hum of electric motors and a soft clunk as it finally shut. The big car, its engine so far away from the passengers as to be virtually silent, eased forward, down the car-lined drive and out into the traffic.

'What's going on?' Nancy asked.

'Didn't you see the way she looked at me?'

'All women look at you like that, Jason. Most of the women at the party would have been only to happy to take you home to bed.'

'No, I mean the way she looked at *us*.'
'Us?'
'Yes. Both of us.'
'Really? She's very lovely. Lovely legs.'
'She's gorgeous.'
'Well then . . .'
'What do you want me to do?'
'Say something.'
'What about Harriet? She works for Harriet.'
'After what you told me about Harriet it's probably her idea.'

They drove up into the canyon, the ocean behind them. Jason used the controls on the little panel in front of him to open the partition again.

'Pull over when you see a good spot. We'd like to get some air.'

'Certainly, sir,' the chauffeuse said, her voice conveying not a hint of anything but politeness.

The car drove on for a few more minutes, past big impressive houses set well back from the road. Then, as the streetlighting disappeared, it pulled off down a small track to the right. The track led to a little copse of trees. Down below, waves crashed into the rocky shoreline. Despite the size of the car it was completely hidden from the road by the trunks and foliage of the trees.

Not hurrying this time, the chauffeuse got out of the car and came round to the passenger door. She opened it and stood in the doorway. The jacket of her black suit had two buttons. Slowly, she undid them one at a time, the light from the interior of the car illuminating her body. She was not wearing a blouse, just a plain white teddy.

The black girl reached behind her back to unzip the skirt. The action pushed her breasts against the white silky material. They were not big but were nevertheless firm and shapely, their nipples hard and prominent. She let the skirt fall to the grass, stepped out of it and stood with her legs apart. The teddy was cut very high on the hip, so high it revealed the crease of her pelvis. The narrow crotch of the garment however exposed not the slightest hint of pubic hair. She was wearing almost transparent hold-up stockings, though their welts were a dark tan, the tight elastic dimpling her thighs.

'You want me to come in there, or do you really want to get some air?' she said in a mocking tone, her voice husky and deep.

'Come in here,' Nancy said putting her hand on Jason's thigh, her fingers curling down into his lap.

The chauffeuse stepped into the car, closing the door after her. As this caused the courtesy light to go out she lent forward to switch on the reading lamp attached to the central door, adjusting it so the light shone into the middle of the car.

On her knees she faced them both, her legs apart, her hands locked behind her head, her elbows raised. In this position she began to undulate her pelvis thrusting it back and forth, the plain while silk of the teddy stretched over it tightly.

Jason watched, fascinated, as the smooth curve of the black girl's sex moved rhythmically with her hips, as though she were being fucked by some invisible lover. He felt Nancy's fingers gripping his thigh more strongly, her eyes locked on the spectacle.

'Is this scenic enough for you?' the chauffeuse said.

'You're very beautiful, aren't you?' Nancy said.

'Watch me . . .' she said, though she could see their eyes were riveted to her body.

She moved her hands down her torso, sliding them over her sides, the silk whispering against her palms. One hand moved on to her breast, cupping it in her palm, while the other slid over the silky canyon of her pubic bone. The plain of her sex between her legs was very wide, enabling her to stroke the whole of her hand back and forth over the silk crotch-piece without bending her fingers inwards.

Nancy's hand undid the zipper of Jason's flies and delved inside. His cock was already hard. She extracted it from the folds of material until it poked out.

'Very impressive . . .' The black girl looked at it as her fingers found the catches that held the crotch of the teddy in place. She snapped them free, crossed both her arms in front of her and pulled the teddy up over her head in one balletic movement.

To Jason's surprise this did not leave her naked. Around her waist was a strip of what looked like rubber, though it was difficult to see properly, its colour so close to the colour of the girl's own skin. This held in place another strip of the same material that ran vertically down the centre of her navel, over her sex and up between her buttocks, to join the waistband again at the back. It was extremely tight fitting and cut deeply into the furrow of her labia. On each side he could see very short pubic hair, hair that was clearly cropped to take away the natural tight curls.

The chauffeuse's hands were concentrating on her nipples. That was another surprise. Both her big bulbous crimson-red nipples had been pierced with small gold rings. The girl's long very thin fingers took hold of each ring and pulled then out and up until her whole breast was stretched by them, the flesh strained and taut. She was looking at Jason as she did it, her eyes full of a peculiar mixture of pain and pride. He could see her body responding, her sexual pulse quickening, her hips undulating again, pushing her sex forward towards him, almost unconsciously.

Letting both breasts go, the girl lent back and felt under the thick wool rug where it had been cut out to accommodate the housing for the cocktail cabinet. Her hand groped around for a moment then came out holding a thin gold chain. With practised ease she clipped the tiny spring-loaded catches at each end of its length into the rings on her nipples. The chain hung free, forming a loop between her breasts.

Wanting to see his reaction to this latest development, the girl looked at Jason, then down to his cock. A tear of fluid had formed at his urethra.

'What's your name?' Nancy asked, her hand wrapped around Jason's shaft, wanking it unhurriedly.

'Augustine,' the girl replied, looking in Nancy's eyes then aiming herself at her, and shaking her breasts, the loop of the gold chain swinging from side to side.

Nancy felt her own nipples pucker. She had never felt them so hard, as if subconsciously she was imagining what it would feel like to be pierced and ringed like this. With her free hand she grasped the bodice of the strapless dress and wrested it over her big breasts. They trembled at their freedom, seeming incredibly white in contrast to the blackness of the girl on her knees.

'Beautiful,' Jason said, looking from Augustine to Nancy. He gathered one of Nancy's breasts in his hand

and squeezed it hard, feeling its wonderful spongy compliance. It made his cock pulse.

Augustine continued her performance. She ran both hands down her sides again, this time smoothing them against her naked flesh. When they reached the thin strip of rubber at her waist, she executed a graceful turn, swinging herself round on the wool rug so her slim buttocks were facing her audience. She dipped her head forward so they were pushed up into the air, the chain at her breasts brushing the rug.

Both her hands came up to the small of her back and unfastened the catch that held the waistband of rubber in place. Then she snaked her right hand down over her belly and up between her legs, covering her sex completely. Her left hand flicked the vertical strip of the odd garment down so it hung between her thighs, held in place now only by the fingers of her right hand. Slowly the right hand slid back, taking the rubber with it revealing first the neat fistula of her anus, then the mouth of her sex.

Another surprise. The lips of the girl's sex were very pink, probably looking pinker in contrast to the dark brown that framed them, but at their centre was not a dark gaping hole. Instead the very pink labia were stretched around the base of a dildo, a thick creamy-coloured dildo, buried to the hilt in her body and obviously held in place by the tight rubber.

Slowly Augustine's fingers gripped the knarled base, contracting her sex to expel it slightly. As soon as she could gain purchase on the end Jason saw her twist it and a muffled humming could be heard. An involuntary moan, guttural and sharp, escaped her mouth which was open wide.

Jason's mind filled with questions. Had she been sitting there all night with the dildo crammed into her sex, the peculiar rubber garment wrapped around her to keep it in place? When had she put the chain under the rug in the back of the car? Was this sexual ballet all prearranged and, if so, by whom? Was the girl acting on her own initiative, inspired by her own desires, or was this Harriet Teitelbaum's idea of making sure Jason had an evening he could never be likely to forget?

Augustine was using one hand to plough the dildo in and out of her body, while the other caressed her thigh above the welt of the hold-up stocking. The hand stroked her black flesh, moving upward, up over the curve of her buttocks, down into the cleft that separated them. Delicately with one finger, she investigated the ring of her anus, as though exploring something she had never felt before, then pushed her finger down into it, driving it in as far as it would go, until Jason could see the web of her other fingers stretched and strained and whitened by the effort. Another guttural moan.

With both hands fully occupied, her next manoeuvre was accomplished with the ease that only comes from constant rehearsal. She rocked her body, so her breasts swung back and forth. The chain from the nipple rings swung too, hitting her navel at one end of their arc and her throat at the other. On the third swing she dipped her head and caught the chain in her mouth. This stopped the oscillation of her breasts immediately, pulling them upwards, the rings biting the tender flesh into which they were sunk.

That was more than Jason could take. It was impossible now to remain just a spectator. He looked at Nancy, her big tits hanging out of the front of her dress. He could see her mouth was slack and her body trembling. She looked back at him with a look of such wild lust in her eyes that he knew she felt exactly as he did.

It was impossible to tell who took the initiative. Did Jason pull Nancy up to her knees, sideways along the bench seat, or did she do it of her own accord? Was she pulling the tight dress up over her buttocks or was he? Who pulled the sheer tights down her thighs?

There was no time – no time to get Jason's trousers off, no time to pull Nancy's tights further down her legs. As soon as Jason saw the hairy labia between her up-turned buttocks, like a vertical mouth grinning at him, he forgot everything else, got astride her legs and pushed his cock into the depths of her cunt. She was wet, steamy and molten. He heard a squelching noise as he rode his cock home.

Augustine was moaning continuously now, her two hands working in tandem between her legs, one pulling the vibrating dildo in and out while the other did the same with her finger, the two plunging in and out together, filling her with choking sensation. At the same time she was sawing her head up and down, her teeth holding the gold chain, pulling on the nipple clips, then letting them relax, the shock of pain the pulling produced timed to coincide with the inward thrusts in her cunt and anus, the feelings of pain and pleasure coalescing, making a melange of feelings that contained elements of both and drove her to an inevitable climax.

Jason was plunging in and out too, his hands holding Nancy's hips, his cock thrusting into her, his balls banging against her closed thighs. In this position her sex seemed tighter, but it was very wet and very excited, her whole body like a live wire. Both of them had their heads turned to the side to watch Augustine.

The interior of the car reeked of sex, was filled with the noise of sex too – the humming of the vibrator in the background, the girl's keening increasingly ardent, moans of pleasure and need, the slurp of wet flesh as Jason powered into Nancy.

They both saw it happen. Her hands stopped moving. Instead they pressed deeper into her body, into both tunnels of her body, pressed with all her muscles straining, her knuckles whitening the black skin, as she wrestled to get the dildo and her finger as high as they could possibly go. At the same time she pulled her head up, making the chain cut into her chin, pulling the nipple rings and her breasts until they were stretched to the absolute limit. Her orgasm was there in her body. It was breaking over the dildo and her finger at the same time, but it was the indefinable sensation from her tits, from her tortured nipples, that was making it engulf her, making it go on and on and on, working its way up from her cunt and arse until it was in her nipples, until finally, she allowed herself the last and greatest pleasure of all, releasing the chain from her mouth, letting her breasts fall free, the surge of relief she felt joined instantly with her orgasm to form some new entity, a monstrous beast of endless appetites.

They both saw it happen, as they were meant to – the tension in her body, the breasts and nipples pulled so tight they thought the nipple rings might be ripped out, then the release, and the shuddering, mind-blowing climax, her breasts quivering, the chain between them swinging loose, her emotions spent.

Jason felt his cock throbbing, spunk pouring into it. Nancy's cunt was pulsing as though a thing apart, a little animal with a toothless mouth, chewing on his cock. He knew it was a product of her excitement. Neither of them had seen anything quite like Augustine's display.

The black girl swivelled round, her turn to watch them. Her eyes went from one to the other, perhaps looking to see who was closer to the borderline. She leant forward and kissed Nancy on the mouth, her tongue pushing between her lips as she ran her hot hand down Jason's buttocks, between his legs until he could feel her fingertips against his balls. Whether it was this, or the sight of the two women's lips – black on white, white on black, writhing against each other so insistently, their tongues vying for position – he did not know or care, but whatever it was, it was enough to push him over the edge. All he cared about was the spunk that was jetting out from his cock and the feeling of Nancy's sex, alive and palpitating around it.

Nancy was coming too, her body as aroused as Jason's by Augustine's performance, and her mouth and tongue kissing her so hotly. She could feel her cunt squirming against his cock, her big breasts hanging down, knocking against each other as Jason rammed into her body. She could feel the black girl sucking at her lips and tongue, sucking harder and stronger as if trying to drawn her out, suck an orgasm out of her. Suddenly she felt Jason's cock kicking inside her and her body spasmed too. She looked down at the nipple rings on the black girl's tits and felt her own nipples knot in sympathy. Then she came, her climax running through her hard nipples and down to her belly and the molten wetness of her cunt, where Jason's spunk mixed with her own spending, and her clitoris pulsed uncontrollably.

Slowly Augustine picked up her clothes, switched off the reading lamp and got out of the car. The courtesy light flashed on and then off again as the heavy passenger door clunked shut. Jason reached forward to pour a glass of champagne. They both badly needed a drink. He sipped the wine appreciatively then handed the glass to Nancy, who had pulled her tights back up around her waist and the bust back over her tits.

'Thanks,' she said, finishing the glass before giving it back to him and wriggling the hem of the dress down over her hips.

'Quite a show...' he said.

Nancy smiled. 'Perhaps I should have my nipples pierced...'

'Mmm... wonder if it hurts.'

'I think I'd like to find out...'

It was dark outside the car but, before she pulled the teddy and the black suit on over her slim figure, Jason was sure he saw the black girl wrapping the odd rubber garment around her body and down between her legs. The cream dildo had already disappeared.

Chapter Eight

The rest of the week passed slowly, neither Jason nor Nancy mentioning the possibilities, or probabilities, of whether Harriet Teitelbaum liked or didn't like the script. Jason tried not to think about it, but with four days to go before the weekend it was difficult not to speculate. Different versions of 'what if' wrote different scenarios in his head.

It was Wednesday morning when the phone rang.

'Can you come to the house? It's important.' The voice belonged to Helen Talbot.

'Now?'

'Yes, now.'

'The beach house?'

'No. Beverly Hills.'

There was only one reason Jason could think of that Helen should invite him to her marital home. She was asking him to perform in front of her husband again.

'It's not what you're thinking,' she said, reading his mind. 'Bill's away.'

'Was that what I was thinking?'

'You know it was.'

He didn't want her to imagine he would have objected. She was using him as much as Hanna had, but certainly wasn't going to make the same mistake and offend her as he had Hanna – that was one lesson he'd learnt the hard way. Helen might only be the wife of a studio boss, not a prime mover like Hanna, but

Jason needed all the friends he could get.

'Helen, you know I wouldn't mind. If it helps you . . .'

'I know that, Jason. It's good of you to say it. But really this is something different.'

'OK.'

'I'll send the car for you. Give me your address. I've only got the phone number.'

He gave her the address without demur.

'I don't think you'll find it a waste of time.'

With that enigmatic remark she hung up.

Ten minutes later a black Rolls Royce Silver Spirit pulled up outside. Jason was ready. He'd had time to shower and put on a fresh shirt. He slammed the front door as the chauffeur, a grey-haired man in his fifties, opened the rear passenger door.

The interior of the Rolls smelt of leather and polish. The driver made no attempt at conversation as he guided the car up the long boulevards to Beverly Hills and through the electrically operated gates of the Talbot's huge mansion.

Helen opened the front door as the car came to a halt in the driveway.

'Hi,' she said, kissing him on both cheeks.

She was wearing a white Lacrosse tracksuit and blue trainers, bright smile on her face. She took Jason's hand and led him into the ultra-modern interior of the house. He had been in the sitting room before but this time she led him through into a small study, very differently decorated from the rest of the house. Here the stainless steel furniture, wooden floors and black lacquered fixtures and fittings that predominated in the other rooms gave way to a cream carpet, chintz curtains and a healthy clutter of books, magazines and ornaments. Closing the door behind them, Helen sat on a large sofa covered in a bright flowery print and patted the cushion next to her indicating that was where he should sit.

As he sat down it would not have surprised him in the least if she'd peeled off the tracksuit and jumped on him.

Instead she asked him if he'd like some coffee. There was a thermos jug on the occasional table in front of them with two cups and saucers. He declined.

'Watch this,' she said, excitement bubbling in her voice.

She picked up a remote control from the table and pointed it at the video recorder and television stacked one on top of the other on a stand in the corner of the room.

The television screen flicked into life.

'I've wound it on to the best bit,' Helen said, her hand resting on Jason's thigh and squeezing it affectionately.

The picture was of an empty room, lit much too brightly and very inexpertly, heavy shadows falling on two walls. There had been some vague attempt to make the room like a prison cell, a grid on the window frame, the single bed a very institutional metal frame, a single dirty blanket its only bedding. To the right of the bed was a door, which again had been painted to look as if it were the door of a prison cell, with a peephole in the upper half.

A man came into shot, pacing up and down on the bare wooden floor. He was dressed in grey fatigue pants and a dirty grey T-shirt. Almost immediately the door was thrown open. A prison guard walked into the cell, a riding crop tucked under his arm. He was dressed in a crude uniform, a grey military-style jacket, not quite matching the grey of his trousers.

The rather crude camera work focused on the prisoner's reaction, an expression of fear in his eyes. The face of the guard was turned away from the camera.

'I told you not to mess with me,' the guard said.

'I didn't.'

'Don't argue with me. You know what you're going to get. You've got to learn I'm the boss in here. Come on, come on. Get bent over.'

With reluctance the prisoner bent over the end of the bed. The guard, his back still to the camera, took a pair of handcuffs, threaded them through the frame of the bed then clipped them round the prisoner's wrists so he couldn't straighten up. He stood behind the man and reached around his waist to untie the draw string of the pants, pulling them down and exposing the prisoner's buttocks.

'My job's not all bad,' the guard said, taking the riding crop in his right hand and caressing the prisoner's buttocks with his left almost affectionately. 'Call out each stroke loud and clear, you hear, boy?'

'Yeah.'

'Yeah what?'

'Yeah, sir.'

The guard raised the crop and swung it down on the man's white buttocks, a swinging stroke that raised an immediate red weal across its path.

'One,' the prisoner intoned

'Not hard enough, was it?' He raised the crop and brought it down much harder this time.

'Two.'

The camera moved around to one side so it could get the prisoner's cock into the frame. It was already beginning to become erect.

'Three.'

The cock throbbed, at full erection on the third stroke. The man's body was tense.

The guard lifted the whip and cracked it down again.

'Ahhh...'

'Say it...'

'Four!' the prisoner gasped.

But instead of raising the whip again the guard threw it down on the bed and tore open the front of his trousers. He wasn't wearing any pants. His cock sprang free, as hard as the prisoner's.

'You want me to stop?' he asked.

'Yes, yes, I'll do anything.'

'You want it, don't you.'

'You bastard, you know I do...'

The guard pushed against the prisoner, the camera swinging around to take in his face for the first time. Jason recognised it at once. The long blond hair and square jaw were unmistakable. It was Al, the Al he had been forced to share Hanna with, the Al who was playing the lead in *The Casting Couch*.

Helen froze the frame of the video recorder.

'Recognise him?'

'Yes.'

'Al Prentiss. He's playing the lead in *The Casting Couch*.'

'And Hanna's bed.'

'Do you want me to go on?'

'I'd rather you didn't.'

She pressed the remote and the television blanked out.

'It's the usual homo gangbang. These things are made real cheap on the amateur circuit. It's usually guys getting off on each other and filming it for extra thrills and extra money. There's always some S and M. This poor guy gets whipped pretty bad but you can see he's really into it.'

'And Al?'

'Al does all the whipping and all the penetration. He's very turned on...'

'Swings both ways. He's obviously giving Hanna what she wants too.' He didn't elaborate on that statement.

'I guessed that much.'

'How did you know?'

'Know what?'

'About *The Casting Couch* and Al playing the lead?'

'It's Bill's picture, remember? His studio. Well, Hanna marched in to him and tells him she's got a great new guy to play the lead. Tells him he's the best thing since instant enchiladas.'

'And?'

'And she tested him. I saw the test. It so happens Honey's with me. Well, Honey knows a lot of people on the wild side. She lived on the wrong side of the tracks for a long time. She says she's seen this guy doing an act in a club she used to go to, a gay joint. Didn't take long to find another example of his work.'

'Well, I suppose it doesn't really matter...'

'What do you mean?'

'After *Escape of the Whores* I've done porn films too.'

'No, Jason,' she said to him patiently, as though

trying to explain something to a small child. 'You don't get the point. Lots of stars started doing mainstream porn films. It's accepted. Marilyn Monroe did it. They say Errol Flynn did. But not gay porn. Gay's different. Gay turns audiences off.'

'I don't see . . .'

'Even if it didn't, Bill wouldn't wear it. He hates gays. Once he see this, Al Prentiss will be history. They'll be back looking for a new star for *The Casting Couth*. Take it from me.'

'What if Hanna insists?'

'Insists on what? On taking her movie to another studio where they'll refuse to finance it too? No one will take Al Prentiss when they find out.'

Jason allowed himself to smile, as confused as he was by all this. Though he couldn't see the difference between what he'd been forced to do and what Al Prentiss had done, clearly, to the important people in Hollywood, there was one.

'So if Hanna has to recast?' he asked tentatively, not liking to hope that was where she was leading.

'Bill liked you, Jason.'

'I went to see Hanna. That's where I met Al.' Again he decided not to go into detail. 'We're back on speaking terms.'

'And fucking terms?' Helen asked bluntly.

'Yes.' There was no point in lying.

'So. I'll show this to Bill. You go and see Hanna. And one and one should make two.'

'You really think so?'

'Trust me.'

'Why are you doing this?'

'I like you, Jason. I think you're a great fuck. And

so does Honey. So, more importantly, does Bill . . .'

'You've helped me already.'

'How so?'

He quickly told her about Harriet Teitelbaum, again admitting the juicy details.

'That's great,' she said when he'd finished. 'So let's hope for a good weekend. Drink now?'

'I'd love one.' Once again Jason felt in need of a drink.

'So would I.'

She got up and went to a small cabinet mounted on the wall. Without asking him what he wanted she poured two glasses of Jack Daniel's, dropped ice into the glass from an ice bucket, carried the glasses back to the sofa and handed one to Jason.

'So here's to prospects,' she said, clinking her glass against his, then knocking back a big slug. Putting the drink on the table, she went to the door and turned the key in the lock.

As she crossed the room again, she unzipped the front of the tracksuit and threw it aside. Her big breasts were naked, unencumbered by a bra. They quivered as she skimmed the tracksuit bottoms off. She wore no panties either.

Standing in front of Jason she stroked her wispy pubic hair.

'I think we should get a bit of practice in, don't you?' she said.

'For what?'

'Oh, Jason. You must know this town by now. Everything is quid pro quo. If Bill throws Al out on his overused backside he'll want a little cooperation if you're going to be reinstated. You know I love my husband. You know I like to please him. And you know what pleases him more than anything in the world, poor guy, is seeing his beautiful blonde, big-breasted, long-legged wife being fucked by some athletic young actor who's just about to become a star. I mean, if Harriet Teitelbaum finances Len's film and you do *The Casting Couch*, you'll be right up there, Jason. And I want you right up me.' The last words made her shudder with excitement.

'What about the servants?'

'You want them to join us?'

'I thought you said, when we first met, you were only unfaithful to your husband when he was watching.'

'I've already broken that rule with you.'

'But not in this house...'

'Jason, there's other ways of watching in this town.'

She glanced up into the corner of the room at ceiling level, then fell to her knees in front of him, unzipping his flies and pulling down his trousers. Jason looked up into the lens of a video camera.

'I'll edit it for him later,' Helen said before sucking Jason's cock into her mouth, feeling it growing instantly as her tongue played around the rim of his glans...

The white double-stretch Cadillac drew up outside Nancy's small house at exactly five to six on Friday. Jason wasn't sure whether he felt disappointed or relieved when he looked out of the window and saw the driver was not Augustine, but a women with a more substantial figure in her fifties, a rather sour expression on her square jowly face.

At exactly six she started to get out of the car and come to the front door but Jason and Nancy were ready, a bag packed for the weekend, and opened the door before she reached it.

'Car for Mr MacIver and Ms Dockery,' the woman said.

'That's us,' Jason said cheerily, smiling broadly but failing to raise a reciprocal reaction from the driver, who merely turned on her heels, went back to the car and stood with the rear passenger door open.

'Good evening,' Nancy said, staring into the Buddha-like face of the woman before she got into the car.

'Good evening, madam,' the chauffeuse replied with studied politeness, taking the case from Jason's hand and putting it on the front seat as soon as he was inside.

In the back of the car everything was as before. The chauffeuse got behind the wheel and announced there was champagne in the fridge should they care for it, just as Augustine had done, then wound up the glass partition. The car pulled out into traffic.

'If she stops in an isolated spot and starts taking her skirt off, we'd better run for it,' Jason said, producing a fit of giggles from Nancy which she had a great deal of trouble controlling.

They did not bother with the champagne which was probably just as well since, after no more than a four- or five-minute ride on the Santa Monica Freeway, the car turned off and came to a halt in the middle of a large airfield, alongside a Belljet Helicopter. The burly chauffeuse came round the car, case in hand, and opened the door for her passengers before handing the case to a smartly uniformed steward who stood waiting.

'I thought we were going to *drive* into the desert,' Nancy said. 'I've never been in a helicopter.'

'Neither have I. Going to be fun.'

'This way, madam, sir,' the steward said, showing them to a ramp of steps that extended from the belly of the aircraft, his walk indicating, to Jason at least, a distinct preference for members of his own sex.

Through the sliding door they found themselves in a small but well-appointed cabin with two sets of airline-style seats facing each other and, like the Cadillac, every conceivable convenience built around them. There was a phone and fax, television and video and repeaters of flight deck information giving their speed, direction, and height. The steward showed them the controls, then retired to the front cabin behind the pilot, showing them how to call him on the intercom if they wanted anything.

As soon as he was gone the whine of the starter motors and the whirl of the rotor blades thrashing the air, stilted at first but soon smooth and slick, vibrated through the whole cabin, and the helicopter began to move forward slightly on its wheels. Seconds later they lifted into the air, almost vertically for fifty feet or so. Then, the nose dipping slightly, they moved to the east, gaining height at the same time.

Below them stretched the huge flat plain of Los Angeles. None of the older houses were built above one-storey in order to avoid earthquake damage, only the massive skyscrapers of Century City, a great cluster of buildings dominated by the black glass towers of the Bonaventure Hotel, rose on the horizon.

They had sat opposite each other and Jason looked at Nancy. She had worn a smart navy blue pinstriped trouser suit, her long hair pleated into a neat tail that hung over its collar, her eyes sparkling with excitement, her big rapacious body making him feel a sudden surge of lust. All the memories of the things they had done together, how her body had responded to numerous provocations, added to his desire. She was an extraordinary creature, her appetites and knowledge of what she liked, honed and sharp. She had taken Jason's experiences, and made them her own. Only last night, for instance, she had demanded to know what had happened with Helen Talbot, wanting to know everything, every last detail, reliving it, making it part of her sexual pleasure and the pleasure she gave him.

They had talked about the weekend. After the display Augustine had given them in the car – which, on reflection, they both agreed had definitely been orchestrated by Harriet Teitelbaum – and Jason's previous experiences with Cynthia and Harriet, they were sure that the weekend in the desert was unlikely to be a purely social event. Both were excited by the prospect. The exotic sexual encounters they had enjoyed recently had been so exceptional that they craved more. This time Jason was going into it with his eyes wide open: he intended to be the user not the used.

Of course, there was the business element too. It would be good to have the uncertainty of Harriet's reaction to the script ended. Judging from the treatment they were being given it was difficult to believe it was not positive but it could be it had a different motivation – perhaps Cynthia's revived interest in Jason or Harriet's obvious fascination with Nancy.

Coming from England, Jason was not used to the seemingly direct connection between sexual favours and business advancement in the film world of Hollywood. At first he had railed against it. Now he had come to accept it, to go with the flow as Nancy had advised him. Now he wasn't at all sure which side of the equation – the sex or the business – he cared about most.

The helicopter had levelled off and was flying at a consistent height over the city. The steward walked through from the front cabin.

'Can I get you anything? We'll be arriving in thirty minutes,' he asked.

'A glass of champagne would be nice,' Nancy said.

'And you, sir?'

'Yes, the same,' Jason replied.

The steward extracted a bottle of Krug 1986 from a small fridge, uncorked it with no fuss and poured it into two flutes, putting the glasses into recesses in the table in front of them and laying out a small plate of hors d'oeuvres that had obviously been specially prepared. The plate was also recessed into the table. There was smoked salmon roulade with cream cheese, tartlettes of fish mousse, tiny blinis topped with belugan caviar and quail's eggs.

'Please call if there's anything else I can get you,' the steward said, going back to the front of the aircraft.

Jason and Nancy sipped the champagne and ate more than a few of the delicious canapés.

'No cabaret today,' Jason said. 'I'm disappointed.'

'Oh, you want the steward to strip for you?'

'He looks as if he might be Al Prentiss's type.'

'He might be like Al Prentiss and swing both ways.'

'You want to try?'

'Only joking. I'm saving myself for later,' she said, eating another piece of smoked salmon.

The scenery outside the windows was changing, the buildings of the city left behind and a desert landscape unfolding. Big boulders and tall cacti were the main features: what greenery there was, which was very little, was concentrated in clumps and looked decidedly sickly. Most of the roads were just dirt tracks, with the exception of one major highway built in an absolute straight line and which the helicopter was following.

Approaching on the horizon, Jason could just see a building, at first not able to make out any details. It was the only building for miles. In fact, apart from the odd broken-down wooden shack and one gas station, it was the only building they'd seen for some time. Jason pointed it out to Nancy.

As they got closer, the helicopter swung left, following a track leading off the main highway. It was then that they saw the full extent of Harriet's desert home and neither of them could quite believe their eyes. Sitting on a rise in the middle of the scrub was an authentic replica of a medieval English castle, complete with castellated battlements, turreted towers, a moat – though not full of water – a portcullis and a drawbridge. As the helicopter flew directly over the thick stone wall they looked down inside the fortifications on to landscaped gardens – an oasis of greenery in the arid waste – a large area of greenhouses, a large kidney-shaped swimming pool – a cascade of water flowing into it at the one end – as well as the rotund of the castle itself. Several people could be seen sitting in the gardens or by the pool, reading or just laying in the sun.

Over the far side of the building, a helicopter pad had been built just outside the moat and to one side of the drawbridge. As softly as a feather, the pilot brought the big machine into land.

Hydraulics deployed the landing steps and the steward escorted them off the aircraft, carrying their case to a small blue electric-powered golf cart that waited at the side of the landing pad. Its driver was a petite auburn-haired girl in a tracksuit, the colour of which exactly matched the colour of the cart.

'Have a good weekend now,' the steward said with more than a hint of innuendo in his voice.

Climbing aboard the rear-facing seat, the car took them down a little ramp and over the drawbridge as the helicopter took off, causing a fierce gust of wind. The sand roundabouts had obviously been cleared because, though the down draught was fierce, there was nothing blowing into their faces.

The car took them under the portcullis into the garden beyond and up to the main doors of the castle itself. The girl took their case.

'This way, please. I'll show you to your rooms,' she said, leading them past a thick oak door and into the vestibule beyond. A curving marble staircase and a crystal chandelier dominated the room. The round walls were hung with yet more modern masterpieces. The floor was marble too, Nancy's high heels clacking on it as they followed the girl up the stairs.

The only thing medieval about the interior was the stone walls. Everything else was modern, with every convenience, including powerful and necessary air conditioning. The castle was deliciously cool in contrast to the sultry heat outside.

Their bedroom was on the first floor, as luxurious as they might have expected. The room was like a suite in a five-star hotel, the pale pink of the carpets reflected in the upholstery of the large sofa and armchair opposite the bed, whose counterpane was a slightly darker red. The walls were rag-rolled in another shading tone. To one side was a separate dressing room, racked with rails and drawers – all empty – and on the other a bathroom, tiled in black and white marble, one wall mirrored from floor to ceiling. There was also a circular bath in the centre of the room, big enough for three or four people and equipped with a jacuzzi. There were double hand basins, a separate shower cubicle and two bidets.

The girl in the blue tracksuit showed them the controls recessed into the bedside tables. The television came out from a concealed panel in the wall and could be swivelled electrically. A different button revealed another panel, behind which was a full bar and refrigerator and the curtains could be opened and closed too, all without moving from the bed.

'If there's anything you want dial nine. The castle's kitchens are open twenty-four hours . . . just like a hotel. The pool outside is kept at a constant eighty-two degrees if you want to swim, but we do advise you to be careful of the sun. It's very powerful in the desert. No pollution to filter it. It's better to use the solariums by the poolside. I hope you enjoy your stay,' she said, closing the bedroom door after her.

Nancy took their case into the dressing room and unpacked the few clothes they had brought.

'Quite a place,' she said as Jason watched her.

'My little place in the desert.' Jason remembered Harriet's description.

'I'd like to see what she thinks is big.'

'And there's lots of other guests.'

They wandered to the main window overlooking the gardens and the pool.

'Going to be interesting,' Nancy said, hugging Jason around the waist.

'Very.'

He swung her round and kissed her full on the mouth.

'Oh sorry . . .' The bedroom door had been flung open and Cynthia barged in. 'Harry's always telling me I've got to remember to knock.'

'Doesn't matter,' Nancy said.

'This is quite a place,' Jason added. 'You remember Nancy?'

'Sure.'

Rather tentatively the two women kissed each other on the cheek. Cynthia was wearing the smallest bikini Jason had ever seen – three yellow triangles at the front, the two on her breasts barely covering her areolae, the one on her belly just hiding the oval of pubic hair, all three held in place by thongs of material so thin they were like string.

'I just came to tell you dinner's at eight and dressy. You've got time for a swim if you want.'

'Sounds good. The helicopter made me hot,' Nancy said.

'I thought that was Jason,' Cynthia giggled. 'Get your things on and I'll show you the way.' Cynthia sat on the big sofa and pulled her legs up under her.

Nancy pulled her jacket off. She could have gone into the dressing room to change but instead she unbuttoned her blouse and stripped it off her shoulders while she stood directly in front of Cyn, knowing the girl was watching her. She unzipped her trousers and let them fall to her ankles stepping out of them, then stooping to pick them off the floor, half turning her back to the young blonde, so she could see the strong curve of her buttocks as she bent over. Straightening up, she faced Cynthia again, reaching behind her back to unclip the three-quarter-cup bra that struggled to contain her big breasts. Then, leaning forward and holding the cups to her breasts with her hands, she shook her shoulders to get the straps to fall over her arms, only then peeling the lacy material from her meaty compliant flesh.

'Nice tits,' Cyn said immediately.

'Thank you.'

'Wish I had tits like that.' Cynthia looked down at her chest.

Nancy wore only a pair of white panties now. Again quite deliberately, she skimmed them down her thighs right in front of Cynthia's eyes. Jason was watching her too, knowing it was her way of making a statement, of establishing her credentials, of telling Cynthia that whatever was going to happen this weekend, she wanted to be part of it.

'Just like me,' Cyn said, staring at Nancy's thickly matted pubic hair. 'But Harry likes me to keep it trimmed.'

'So I see,' Nancy said looking back into Cyn's lap, the neat oval of pubic hair overlapping the yellow material.

'Do you like that?' Cyn asked.

'I love it,' Nancy said. 'But then I love most things...'

As if by way of demonstration, she shook her breasts from side to side. They made a slapping noise as they smacked against each other. With that she turned and went to find her swimsuit in the dressing room.

'She's very sexy,' Cyn said.

'Very,' Jason agreed pulling his jacket and shirt off. Nancy's display had made his cock unfurl. It poked through his boxer shorts as he pulled his trousers down.

'Well, look at that.'

'Has he got an erection again?' Nancy said, her black one-piece swimsuit pulled up only as far as her waist. 'I can't keep it down.' She tugged the straps of the swimsuit up over her arms and smoothed it over her breasts.

'The water'll cool him down,' Cynthia said, as Nancy gave Jason his swimming trunks, her eyes never leaving his cock as he replaced the shorts with the trunks. They only just covered his erection.

Jason was a little surprised that Cynthia had not taken advantage of his condition, that the two women had not abandoned the idea of swimming in favour of the large double bed, but Cynthia got up, and without a further word, led them through the castle, down long corridors of bedrooms, to a small staircase which led past shower rooms and saunas, then, eventually out into the open by the pool.

The pool was deep, its water clear and warm, the artificial waterfall at one end spraying positive ions into the air that seemed to relieve the stifling heat.

There were several people lying, mostly in couples, around the edge and Jason thought he recognised one or two faces from the party. Under an awning at the end opposite the waterfall, a bar had been set up where a barman and a waitress, in a skimpy, tight-fitting high-cut red swimsuit, were stationed to cater for the guests.

Cynthia led them over to a group of empty loungers under a circular canvas sunshade. Each lounger had a white bath towel neatly folded on its white-and-blue striped cushions.

While Cynthia arranged herself in the shade, Nancy dived into the pool, closely followed by Jason. They swam energetically, racing each other up and down the long pool, swimming underwater, occasionally playful, but more often taking their exercise seriously, stretching their muscles and making themselves work hard. They paid little attention to the other guests, none of whom came into the water.

It was only when Jason finally lifted himself out and ran to the lounger to pick up a towel that he noticed a white-haired man lying on a double lounger, almost the width of a small double bed. Though he couldn't put a name to his face it was, he knew, an actor he recognised from countless television shows and movies. A small petite blonde was kneeling on the lounger beside him, her mouth impaled on his cock, her hand juggling with his balls.

As Nancy got out of the pool too, Jason directed her attention to the spectacle with a nod. But that was, he soon realised, not the only activity. Across the other side of the pool two women lay, the tops of their bikinis abandoned, each with one hand buried in the panties of the other, not doing much, just resting there, a finger no doubt pressed against the other's clitoris.

Sitting back on the lounger, between Cyn and Nancy, Jason saw that most of the eight or nine people around the pool were engaged in some sort of leisurely sexual exploration. A man, yet another face Jason vaguely recognised from films, and a long-haired blonde lay on a single-sized lounger on their sides. The man's hands cupped her breasts and her buttocks spooned into his navel, his cock hard between her legs, their swimwear discarded on the tiled terracing. The heat, and it was still hot even in the shade, made energetic completion too much effort; that, no doubt, would come later. For the time being the guests appeared content to take their pleasure slowly, enjoying the extra spice of exhibitionism, aware of the eyes of the others watching their activities.

Jason exchanged a look with Nancy. What they had anticipated from their weekend was already coming true.

'You don't mind, do you?' Cynthia said, getting to her feet. She was looking down into Jason's lap. 'I fancy a little hors d'oeuvre before dinner...'

'Why should I mind?' Nancy replied as the question had been directed at her, Jason's opinion was clearly irrelevant.

Cynthia tugged Jason's trunks down to his thighs. He cooperated, raising his buttocks off the cushion. She didn't bother to take them all the way down, leaving them as soon as they were clear of his cock. Then she swung herself over him to kneel above his legs and dipped her head, sucking his flaccid cock into her mouth. Instantly Jason felt himself growing hard.

Nancy got up, went to the back of Jason's lounger, pulled the bar holding the backrest at an angle out of the way and lowered it so Jason was lying flat.

'Just to show willing,' she said, grinning as she climbed over Jason's face. She held the crotch of the swimsuit aside and lowered her sex on to Jason's mouth, facing Cyn so she could watch the urchin-like blonde with her spiky coarse hair working on his cock. As Jason tasted Nancy's labia, he felt his cock come to full erection, Cynthia's tongue circling the rim of his glans. Like all the other guests around the pool neither woman appeared to be in any hurry. Nancy responded to his long licks languidly, while Cyn, having achieved her objective, unknotted the side of the tiny bikini pants, pulled them away and slowly sank her sex on to his phallus.

'Having a good time, girls?'

Jason could just glimpse the long legs and high-heeled slippers of the woman who had come to stand by the lounger. Though he could not see her face she was obviously looking at what was going on.

'Umm...' he heard Cyn reply. 'You want a piece?'

'No... saving myself for later.' Her attention had obviously turned to Nancy. 'You're new. Nice tits.'

The woman ran her hand down Nancy's neck and cupped one of her swimsuited breasts in her hand, squeezing it slightly. Jason felt Nancy's body react with excitement.

'Hasn't she got nice tits, Irving?'

A pair of male feet in leather sandals appeared at the side of the lounger.

'Nice legs, too. Is he giving you a good time?'

'He's very good,' Nancy said, trying to keep her voice

steady and finding it difficult. The casualness with which these total strangers were treating this encounter was turning her on. Their eyes devouring her body, clearly working out what it would be like to touch and kiss and fuck her. She could see the woman, a flaming redhead, looking at the way Jason's cock was sliding lazily in and out of Cynthia's thick pubic hair. She could see the man's eyes on the crotch of her swimsuit where she held it aside. She didn't know why, but it was their total lack of concern, as though this was something they saw and did every day, that excited her so.

'Come on, Irving. Let's get changed. Any more of this and I'll want to join in.'

'Sure, honey,' Irving said, his cock firm in his tight red trunks.

'I certainly hope we'll see you later,' the redhead said. She was about to walk away when she turned, hooked her hand around Nancy's neck and kissed her full on the mouth, pushing her tongue deep between Nancy's lips. She broke the kiss without a word and walked away.

Cynthia climbed off Jason. There was an audible squelch.

'They're right. We'd better go. Harry likes everyone dressed up to the nines for dinner, me included.'

'Who's that woman?' Nancy said, pushing herself down on to Jason's mouth for one last touch.

'One of the regulars.'

Nancy got up with reluctance, the excitement created by the strangers not easy to ignore.

Jason sat up, turning to see the couple walking away, the man's hand flitting over the redhead's buttocks, the design of her swimwear leaving only a thong between them, the big ovals of meaty flesh swinging from side to side as she walked. Jason's cock pulsed.

'Regulars?' Nancy asked.

'Regular weekenders... friends of Harry's. So I'll see you later. Eight on the dot. Harry's going to be waiting for you.' Playfully she stooped, grabbed Jason's cock and pretended to talk to it. 'See you later too,' she said. She picked up her bikini bottoms but did not bother to put them on again.

'Hey, wait for us,' Jason said. 'I'm not sure how to get back.'

He hopped to his feet, pulling his trunks back up and taking Nancy's hand. They followed Cynthia back into the house. His erection was still hard, and grew harder still, as he passed the man and woman lying on their side. Another blonde had joined them, pressing herself into the man's back so he was sandwiched between two sensuous blondes.

'Pretty,' he said.

'Very,' Nancy replied, squeezing his hand tightly.

Chapter Nine

The temptation to throw Nancy down on the big bed, in fact to pull Cynthia down too as she'd escorted them right back into their bedroom still wearing only the miniscule bikini bra, was enormous, but Jason resisted it. Instead he had gone straight to the bathroom and climbed under the shower where, at long last, his erection had wilted.

At exactly five to eight Jason, dressed in his dark Armani suit and silk shirt, this one with a Sulka silk tie, was inspecting Nancy's outfit. She wore a long flame-red backless dress with a halter neck formed into a collar around her throat. The side of the skirt was split, revealing glimpses of her thigh. In fact, because of not being able to wear a bra, Nancy did not usually go in for backless dresses, but she had brought this one specially for the occasion, knowing the sides of her breasts could be seen when she moved her arms, their weight and size only too obvious.

'Well?' she asked.

'Edible,' Jason said, meaning it. He moved to kiss her neck. She had her hair pinned up, so the red collar of the halter was emphasised against her fair skin.

They walked down the long corridor to the marble staircase and as they started down slowly, because of the height of Nancy's heels, Harriet Teitelbaum appeared at the bottom, a dinner jacket and black bow tie effectively hiding anything that might suggest she was a woman.

'My dears,' she said as they were halfway down, 'you must forgive me for not greeting you personally on arrival. Business, I fear. Always the same story.'

As soon as they were in range, she took Nancy's hand and kissed it. Jason could see her eyes had been devouring Nancy's body, particularly her thigh as the skirt had been kicked open on the way down. It was not difficult to read what was going on in her mind.

'A beautiful companion,' Harriet said to Jason. 'Quite beautiful.' She took Nancy's arm.

'Thank you.' He couldn't think of anything else to say.

'Please, this way . . .'

With Nancy's arm firmly tucked into hers, Harriet lead the way into a palatial sitting room, where ten or eleven people were standing around chattering, as a waitress plied them with glasses of champagne. Some of the men wore black tie, others, like Jason, suits, but none were casually dressed. The women, without exception, wore elaborate and expensive haute couture, some modest, some outrageously décolleté.

'Champagne? Krug. My favourite.'

The waitress appeared at Harriet's side immediately. They both took a glass, though Harriet did not. 'Now, who don't you know?'

Jason spotted Cynthia in a corner talking to the redhead he'd seen by the pool. She was wearing another Parisian creation, this time a Gautier – a satin corset with bra cups like ice-cream cones, high-heeled satin thigh boots attached to the corset by suspenders, both in baby pink worn over crimson opaque tights. The redhead caught his eye and smiled as he was introduced to a Senator from Florida and his much younger wife. They were quickly introduced to all the other guests, leaving the redhead until last.

'And this is Maisy Duke. Where's Irving?'

'Just gone to pee,' Maisy said. 'Very pleased to meet you,' she said to Jason, shaking his hand, her eyes roaming Nancy and Jason equally as if trying to imagine them without clothes again. She kissed Nancy on the cheek after their introduction.

'We meet again,' Irving Duke said reappearing.

'Irving's into space,' Harry said as he shook Jason's hand.

'NASA space, not real estate,' he said laughing.

'And his wife's into anything with a pulse. Isn't that right, Maisy?' Harriet asked.

'Or they're into me. And these two are welcome additions to our little circle,' Maisy said. 'Harriet always has such good taste. Everyone here's handpicked. You're very privileged to get an invitation...'

'Privileged if you're a man, beautiful if you're a woman,' Irving added. 'And to be privileged you have to be a success.'

It was true. All the women in the room were stunning and some were famous. All the men were stars in some field – films, politics or sport. There were three actors, a man who ran the largest public relations firm in LA and another whose company was the biggest computer software manufacturer in the whole country. All presumably had one thing in common – a very liberal attitude to sexual relationships.

Jason was trying to decide if he should bring up the question of the script. But, just as he worked out what he was going to say, Harriet took Nancy over to talk to the software manufacturer.

'So, you're an actor,' Maisy Duke said. 'You're obviously going to be a star or you wouldn't be here.' Her husband had drifted away and they were alone in one corner of the big room.

'I don't know about that.'

'Sure you do . . .'

He saw Maisy's eyes looking at him again, a lascivious, lecherous look. She raised an eyebrow, a gesture that begged a question, then smiled, showing two rows of gleaming, very equally shaped teeth, behind fleshy, very red lips.

'Dinner, I think,' Harriet said loudly from across the room. Taking Nancy's arm once again, she led the way through a pair of walnut doors into the dining room. As the couples filed through, Jason found Cynthia on his arm.

'Maisy's got the hots for you,' she said.

'What's going on here, Cyn?' he asked.

She smiled. 'You'll see.'

The dining room was dominated by a huge gothic fireplace where logs the size of tree trunks burnt merrily in the hearth. The air conditioning had been turned up higher in this room to make its flames seem necessary. An oval table stood in the middle of the room, its surface covered in white linen, shining solid-silver cutlery and a line of crystal glasses set for each course, tiny, precisely arranged flower displays in front of each guest, silver candelabra holding big cream candles that flickered in the dimmed light from an overhead chandelier.

Nancy was escorted by Harriet to the head of the table to sit at her right hand while Jason was placed at the other end on Cynthia's left, indicating that they were the guests of honour.

Almost the second Harriet sat down, a frock-coated butler and several waitresses began to serve dinner. A chilled soup of artichokes was followed by a mousse of lobster wrapped in spinach, a sorbet made from Calvados, and a fillet of beef in a rich red-wine-and-truffle sauce. A *vacherin* of meringue and *fraise des bois* on large black plates, sprinkled with icing sugar to resemble a dusting of snow, was served for dessert.

Jason chatted amicably enough to Cynthia and Maisy Duke, who was seated at his end of the table, and watched Harriet at the other end, talking ever more animatedly to Nancy, her hand often covering Nancy's and squeezing it to emphasise a point.

As a series of wines were served with each course, each poured into a different-sized glass, Jason felt his mood change. He had assumed this weekend was going to contain an element of sex but that it would also lead to a discussion of Len Furey's script. But, as he looked around the table and thought back to the conversation before dinner, he experienced a feeling he had had so many times before in his short time in Hollywood. He was being used. Harriet had held out the bait and he had taken it – now she held her line up, determined to make him wriggle and squirm, to make him do anything before he would find out whether she was prepared to put up the money for the film. The desert castle was run like a exclusive club for its very exclusive members to indulge their sexual proclivities. Jason and Nancy had been brought along as new young blood, to add variety to jaded palates.

Jason had already been involved in one of Harriet's more bizzare sexual scenarios, the basement 'theatre' in her apartment block, probably well known to the habitués of the castle. How many of the company at the table had watched him that night, he wondered? This weekend, he was becoming more and more convinced, was going to be more of the same. The party at the museum had not been anything to do with the script. Harriet's interest in Jason had been revived by his session with Cynthia – no doubt related to her in every detail. Her instant fascination with Nancy had added extra spice.

If he was right, if their interest in the script was no more than a means to an end, he wanted to know.

'Did you read the script?' he asked Cynthia abruptly, as little silver two-tiered plates of petits fours were distributed among the guests and coffee arrived, served from steaming Georgian silver pots.

'You know I did, Jason. I told you it was great.'

'And?'

'Harriet's going to talk to you about it later.'

'How much later?'

'What's this?' Maisy interrupted. 'Another porn job? You were great in the last one, darling. I watched it twice all the way through. That scene where you're tied to the tree . . .'

'You've seen it?' Jason said. As far as he knew the film was still not finished.

'Harry got us a private copy. I'm thinking of tying Irving to a tree.'

'When are we going to talk about the script?' Jason persisted. He wondered if Harriet had sent copies of *Escape of the Whores* to all the guests so they could see what they were getting, an aperitif to the main event.

'Later,' Cyn said firmly.

'Tonight?'

'Not tonight,' Maisy said. 'No one's going to do much more talking tonight Jason...'

'It's a great script, Jas... I told Harry that,' Cyn said ignoring Maisy.

'And?' Jason was not prepared to let it go.

'And she wants to talk to you about it.'

'To say what?'

'Jason, what's got into you? Relax. We've got all day tomorrow. Why do you think she's invited you here?'

'To get fucked,' Jason said, looking Cynthia straight in the eyes.

'Right,' Maisy said.

'Sure,' Cyn said. 'But you knew that. Jesus, you wanted to fuck me the other day. You changed your mind? No one's forcing you. What do you think this is?'

'Don't you want to fuck me?' Maisy said, looking disappointed.

Cynthia was right, of course. Both Nancy and he had come knowing what was likely to be on the agenda and it had excited them when, by the pool, it had been confirmed. There hadn't been a moment to talk privately with Harry and, as Cynthia said, tomorrow they would have all day. Jason took a sip of the dessert wine that had been poured into the last of the line of glasses – an orange muscat from the Quady Vineyards in Napa Valley – and tried to be more positive, telling himself it was his treatment by Hanna that had made him over-sensitive to abuses of power. He needed to relax. Whatever was going to happen tonight was not going to be exactly unpleasant. They were here now and might as well enjoy it.

'You're right,' he said to Cynthia quietly.

Several of the guests had left the table. Irving, Maisy's husband, had come over, whispered something in her ear and had taken her off too. The people who remained ordered brandy or liqueurs of various sorts and talked languidly.

'So, would you like a guided tour of the mystery castle?' Cynthia said.

Jason looked over at Nancy at the other end of the table. She was talking animatedly to Harriet, gesturing with her hands to explain some agreement. It was difficult to remember Harriet was a woman, so little about her appearance suggested any kind of femininity. To the casual observer it looked as though Nancy was being flattered and charmed by an attentive man.

'What about Nancy?' he asked.

'Harry'll look after her, don't worry.'

For a second Jason felt a flash of jealousy, but told himself that was ridiculous after everything they had been through together. Nancy was more than capable of looking after herself.

Taking his hand, Cynthia led him out of the dining room and into the hall. Guiding him down a long passageway under the main staircase, she showed him the gymnasium, fully equipped with all the latest machines, and the indoor pool, much smaller than the one outside but still a good size.

On again Cynthia showed him the greenhouses he had seen from the air. There were three separate areas each at a different temperature. The first was used for growing vegetables, neatly planted with salad plants, peppers and melons. The second was entirely devoted to flowers and was much hotter. Tropical orchids and all sorts of exotica grew here in every imaginable colour and shape. At the far end, the greenhouse was filled with butterflies, an astonishing collection, some the size of a dinner plate, others no bigger than a thumbnail, their colours as varied as the flowers had been.

'Pretty, aren't they?' Cyn said.

'Harriet's idea?'

'Oh yes. There's some very rare species.'

It was a fascinating collection but not, Jason knew, the main reason the guests came to the castle.

'So, where has everyone disappeared to?' he asked. There was no one else in the greenhouses and no-one outside by the pool either.

'You weren't interested, remember?' Cyn teased.

'I didn't say that. Come on. Give me the rest of the tour,' he said, scooping her slight frame into his arms and kissing her full on the mouth.

'And I thought you didn't fancy me any more,' she mocked.

'No you didn't.'

They walked back through the greenhouses and into the castle. Cynthia led the way back down the passage but halfway to the main staircase she stopped at a heavy wooden door. On the side of its frame was a computer lock into which she programmed a three-number sequence. The door opened to reveal a small lift. Cynthia pressed the call button and the stainless-steel doors slid open immediately.

'Going down,' she giggled as Jason got in besides her.

There was only one button on the control panel.

Jason felt a familiar sinking feeling as the lift descended one floor.

The stainless-steel doors slid open to reveal what looked like the changing room in a top-class health club. To one side was a bank of showers, in the middle a line of slatted wooden benches and, on the other, racks of clothes hanging in steel baskets. Jason recognised a couple of the dresses he had seen earlier.

'If you want to go in you have to strip,' Cynthia said, unhooking one of the long metal baskets from the ceiling rail where they hung, their upper edge shaped like a coat hanger.

'In where?'

'There . . .' she said unhelpfully, indicating a large black door at the end of the room. 'Come on, trust me . . .'

Jason sat on one of the wooden benches. He watched as Cynthia undid the suspenders that held the satin thigh boots to the corset and pulled them off. He wondered what lay behind the black door, though he had a pretty good idea.

'Unzip me,' Cyn said, turning her back so Jason could get at the long zipper that ran down the back of the corset. 'For women it's optional. Stripping, I mean. The women can wear whatever they like . . .'

She pulled off the corset and the tights. She wasn't wearing panties. 'No one's forcing you,' she said, sensing a hesitancy in him.

No one was, of course. But would the promised conference on the script take place if he said no? That was a question that would never be answered, as he had no intention of refusing. Another emotion was starting to assert itself, one that overrode his other concerns. He looked at Cynthia, her little pert breasts and bottom, her waif-like face, and felt a knot of desire form in his stomach. He thought of this afternoon by the pool, of the women at dinner, all very different in type but all, without exception, extremely beautiful. What had Irving said? 'Privileged men, beautiful women.' Behind that black door there was little doubt he would be privileged to join a very exclusive club.

He searched the racks of clothes, looking for Nancy's dress, thinking Harriet may have brought her down here while they were in the greenhouses. On the other hand, she may have kept her dress on and there was certainly no way of telling Harriet's dinner jacket from any of the other men's.

'Is Nancy here?' he asked.

'I don't know . . .' Cyn answered. 'Maybe.'

While Jason stripped out of his clothes and hung them on the metal frame, Cynthia went to a small cupboard by the black door. She extracted two items and came back to where Jason stood naked.

'Sit again,' she said.

'What is it?'

'This *is* compulsory for everyone,' she said, standing behind him. She took the grey hood, opened it and pulled it down over his head. It was made from an odd material, slick and smooth and tautly elasticated like a nylon Lycra but with the appearance of leather. It has oval slits for eyes, nose and mouth but otherwise enclosed the head completely. Cynthia pulled it down, adjusting the slits to fit his features, then pulling the laces that tightened it at the back. Satisfied, after two or three sharp tugs, that it fitted as snugly as it could, she tied off the cords.

'Now me,' she said holding up a second hood, this one a dark blue, and sitting on the bench. Jason fitted the hood over her bleached-blonde hair and her chalky make-up. He did it rather less expertly than she had, but finally managed to get it into place, the lacing pulling the material so tightly into her features it even followed the contours of her cheekbones and jaw, moulding itself completely to her face.

'It's just a precaution,' she explained.

'Against what?'

'A lot of famous faces. Someone could make a lot of money from a photograph, couldn't they? One of the women might try and smuggle something in . . . It's a big temptation.'

'But upstairs . . .'

'Upstairs they were just having dinner. This way no one can get anything. And it's quite sexy, don't you think?'

Cynthia went to the black door. There was another computer lock into which she keyed a sequence of numbers. The door lock buzzed and opened.

'Well . . . ?' She held her hand out to take Jason's, then swung the door wide open and led him through.

The first thing he saw was a naked woman. From the brief glimpse he had had of her body this afternoon, and from the fact she had flaming-red pubic hair, he guessed the woman was Maisy Duke, but the dark green mask over her head made it impossible to be sure.

Whoever the woman was, she was stretched out like a cross, her arms spread out and suspended from metal rings attached to a beam that ran the width of the room, her legs parted and tied to identical rings set in

RETURN TO THE CASTING COUCH

the stone-flagged floor. Three men, all hooded, all naked, and all erect were giving her their full attention. Two stood in front of her, one kneading and pummelling her breasts, varying his touch from light and gentle to hard and painful, the other holding a curved wooden dildo between her legs. The dildo was shaped like a scimitar and its base flared out to prevent too great a penetration. The man plied it to and fro in her body.

The third man stood behind her, his cock obviously inserted in her anus, pounding into it unremittingly, his hands holding on to her hips. Jason thought this might well be Irving but again could not be sure. He was very near to orgasm, and so was she, judging from the inarticulate exclamations that escaped from both their mouths. The man's fingers dug deeper and deeper into her fleshy flanks, holding her more and more tightly, forcing her to where he needed her to be, his hips propelling him like a steam hammer. Then his body went rigid, he stopped moving, gasped twice as though he was having trouble breathing, his hands hanging on to her for dear life, before his eyes closed and his muscles went slack.

But Maisy, if that was who the woman was, held herself back. Her eyes burning with excitement, were looking straight at Jason. It was not difficult to see what they were telling him. She must have been in pain, stretched out as she was, but the pain had been translated by the heat of sex to all-consuming pleasure. She wanted more. And she was going to get it.

The man in front of her, who had been manipulating her breasts, went over to the far wall. Hanging from the side was a long-lashed whip. Taking it down he practised a stroke with it, the lash whistling through the air.

'This is what she wants,' he said.

'Yes,' Maisy confirmed, wriggling her sex on to the hard wooden shaft still held firmly in her body. 'Give it to me . . .'

Thwack. The sound of leather rippling across her pliant buttocks filled the air. Jason saw the woman's eyes flutter open again, even more excited than before. He was certain it was Maisy. She twisted against her bonds, squirming her hips from side to side, looking straight at Jason as she'd looked at him upstairs, wanting to come for him.

Thwack. The second stroke was enough. It burnt into her body like a brand. As the hot pain surged through her, it electrified her already taut nerves and plunged her over the edge, her sex contracting on the hard wooden phallus, her mind filled with so many sensations it was simply overwhelmed.

Cynthia tugged on Jason's arm. 'There's a lot more to see,' she said quietly.

Another man had come up behind Maisy, his cock knarled, ugly and very big. As the man withdrew the wooden shaft, he inserted his cock into her sex, reaming up into her, giving her no time to rest. From the expression in her eyes she wanted none either, the hot pulsing phallus a marvellous contrast to the artificial version.

Jason had been so rapt in the spectacle right in front of him, he had not really taken in the rest of his surroundings. They were standing in what looked like a medieval dungeon – a brick-vaulted ceiling with stone walls and floor, the whole room lit by cast-iron chandeliers with endless numbers of long white candles stuck into the prickets on their circular frames. The walls were hung with metal rings and various antique, at least they looked antique, devices of torture – thumbscrews, and chest straps and metal balls and chains, as well as more modern, and well used, whips and paddles, tawses and ferules. Three wooden beams crossed the ceiling, all hung with bondage equipment, like the chains that held Maisy so firmly. One looked like a playground swing, another like a hammock.

On the floor there was a replica of a medieval rack and a simple slatted wooden bed amply provided with anchorage points into which a victim could be effectively bound. There was an odd-shaped chair too, with numerous leather straps screwed to its frame, its seat largely hollowed out.

Aside from the men surrounding Maisy, there were only three other occupants of the dungeon, two women and a man. The man had been chained to the overhead beam, his hands bound together and stretched up over his head. One of the women – her body slender and fine-waisted, her legs long and exquisitely shaped – was applying what looked like a big table-tennis bat to the man's buttocks, already so red they were crimson. The other woman, much shorter but with a body no-less-finely proportioned, had one arm wrapped around the man's waist while her other hand circled his cock, wanking it with what Jason thought was probably maddeningly light touches.

A leather gag had been inserted in the man's mouth and tied around his dark burgundy-coloured hood. He seemed to be trying to say the word 'please' over and over again.

The tight hoods on the two women, both black, had the effect of concentrating attention on their bodies and on their eyes. The woman applying the paddle had dark green eyes. She was wearing a catsuit made from sheer nylon, her big breasts squashed by its tightness, her auburn pubic hair crushed flat. The woman teasing his cock was naked but for a pair of very black hold-up stockings and high-heeled shoes.

How long they intended to go on torturing the man Jason didn't know, but as he watched they seemed to sense he was getting too near the point of no return and the shorter of the two women took her hand away completely, provoking a muffled moan of despair from their victim.

Cynthia pulled Jason's hand, leading him on. He saw another black door set in the wall opposite the one they had entered by. As they approached it, he looked back over his shoulder at the two bound figures. He suddenly remembered Helen Talbot tied to the bench in the black room in her beach house, her legs spread, her arms bound. He wondered if she was a member of Harriet Teitelbaum's inner circle, privy to the secrets of the dungeon. Was that why she had suggested he go and see Harriet again?

Cynthia punched numbers into a third computer lock. The door opened and she piloted Jason through.

Jason found himself in a long wide room. Unlike the dungeon this area was normally furnished, carpeted with a deep-pile beige carpet, its walls covered in a rich oatmeal-coloured silk. Obviously, there were no windows and only the one door through which they'd entered. The room was furnished with a number of beds, a couple of singles but mostly doubles, all covered in black silk sheets. Above, on the ceiling, a spotlight lit each bed, its beam carefully focused to include only the area of the bed itself, the light not spilling over on too much of the floor, giving each bed the appearance of a stage on which one was expected to perform.

Several of the beds were occupied with several different performances. Looking round, Jason searched for Nancy. Even though everyone was hooded, hers was not a body he would fail to recognise. He took Cynthia's hand, this time leading her from bed to bed examining the women. Nancy was not among them.

Whereas the dungeon was intended for guests who were interested in S and M, the pursuits in this room were more conventional. As he roamed around, though, he did notice some of the participants had been bound in various ways, but nothing like as cruelly as the examples outside. Many of the men wore harnesses of leather around their cocks and balls, and many of the women, black nipple clips. Not all the women were naked, some had their dresses pulled over their hips, others wore lingerie, and most still wore high heels.

'Jason...' Cynthia whimpered like a dog looking at a large bone but unable to get at it. She sat on one of the unoccupied double beds.

'Is there another room?'

'Forget Nancy...' she said, reading his mind. 'Look at that, doesn't that turn you on?'

He followed her gaze. In the white light of the spotlight, a few feet away on the next bed, a fleshy woman, her breasts big and proud, was kneeling between the legs of a man, who was plunging his cock in and out of her mouth. Another woman, of much slimmer build, pushed her mouth up between the first woman's knees to get at her sex.

Up until this point Jason had viewed what he had been shown like a sexual Disneyworld. He was fascinated but not involved, not wanting to go on any of the rides.

He was also worried about Nancy. He'd expected to find her down here, indulging her appetites, suspecting this would be very much to her taste. That she was not made him think Harriet had other plans for her. What Nancy's attitude to Harriet's advances would be he did not know, that was something they hadn't discussed, but Harriet had used him and he didn't want Nancy to be put in the same position.

'What's happening to Nancy?' he asked Cyn.

'Nothing, Jason. Harriet'll look after her.'

'That's what worries me.'

'Trust me, Jason. It's all right.'

'You promise?'

'Promise.' She looked completely sincere.

Well, he thought, Nancy is a big girl and, he hoped, quite capable of handling whatever Harriet Teitelbaum had in mind for her.

'Jason . . .' Cyn whined impatiently, deciding to adopt a more direct approach and dropping to her knees to gobble his cock into her mouth and suck on it hard. 'Mmm . . . love your cock . . .' she muttered as she moved her mouth under his shaft to suck his balls.

'Is this a private party or can anyone join in?'

Jason felt a full, rich big-breasted body slide against his back. Long slender arms reached around him, one cradling his chest, the other moving up to his cheek, turning his head around so he could be kissed. Her hooded face was anonymous but her mouth was open, a somehow obscene gash, wet and red against the grey hood she wore. He looked into her dark brown eyes, through the oval slits, and felt her sucking his tongue in as she pressed her breasts, the nipples as hard as stone, into his shoulderblades.

Cynthia got back on the bed. She lay on her back and opened her legs, bending her knees right back until she could grasp her ankles in her hands. She pulled them back even more, splitting herself, revealing her sex so Jason could see, below the neatly cut oval of pubic hair, the open mouth of her glistening wet cunt.

'Fuck me, Jas.'

The woman behind let him go. He knelt between Cynthia's legs, looking down at her pussy, her labia spread open so much he could see the little knot of her clitoris, pink and exposed.

The woman in the grey hood knelt up on the bed alongside Cyn's chest. She was wearing a red suspender belt which held red stockings tautly against her long legs, and red high heels. Her full ovoid breasts were topped by knob-like nipples and a dark brown areola. Her buttocks were as voluptuous as her breasts, rich ripe curves divided by a deep canyon. Her pubic hair was sparse and very short, each hair of the triangle of her belly pointing to the apex of her thighs. Her labia were virtually hairless, every line and detail clearly visible. Her thighs, bisected by the welts of the stockings, were meaty too, especially in this kneeling position, her muscles taut, her heels resting on her bottom.

Reaching forward, her hands cupped Cynthia's breasts, fingers pinching the nipples.

'Fuck her,' she said. 'You can see she needs it.'

Jason's cock was throbbing. He lay out, supporting himself on his arms, one arm between the kneeling woman's thighs, and used his hips to push his penis into the open lips of Cyn's cunt.

'Umm . . .' she responded.

He pushed forward, feeling her wetness.

'Does she feel good?' the woman asked.

'Yes . . .' he moaned.

'Make her come. We'll make her come.' The woman took one hand from Cyn's breasts. She stroked it down Jason's back, making him shudder, her touch like electricity. The hand passed over her buttocks, down between his legs, until he felt her fingers on his balls, juggling them, reeling them into her grasp, so she could hold them both firmly in her hand.

As soon as this was accomplished her other hand tweaked Cynthia's breast hard – so hard Jason could feel it produce a shudder of pleasure in Cyn's body that made her sex contract around him – then she worked it down between their bodies, worming it against their navels until the fingers could reach Cynthia's clitoris. Jason could feel it beginning to move and, instantaneously, felt Cyn tremble.

'Fuck her then,' the woman chided.

He looked into her dark brown eyes, shining out from the grey hood. He would love to have torn the hood away and seen her face. He could see her tongue darting out between her lips.

He began to move, feeling the woman pulling at his balls, while her other hand, flat between their bellies, managed to move enough to nudge Cynthia's swollen clit from side to side.

'Oh, that's so gooood . . .' Cynthia moaned.

'Nice cock, is it?'

'Very hard...'

The woman's breast pressed against Jason's upper arm. He turned his head and caught her nipple between his teeth without stopping the rhythm of his hips, nipping it hard before he released it. He felt her hand tighten on his balls by way of response.

Cynthia was melting under him, her wrists still hanging on to her ankles, the depths of her cunt open to him, his hard long shaft ploughing into her, stretching her sex in every direction, its tip probing deeper and deeper as she felt herself opening, all resistance gone. She didn't know who was affecting her most, the anonymous grey-masked woman whose fingers touched her so beautifully, or Jason, bent over her, his eyes looking into hers, his muscled body on top of her as hard as his cock inside.

'Coming...' was all she could say as the feelings flooded over her and her body went rigid, every nerve involved, all wanting to be part of the finale, all eager to join the chorus of sensation that peaked in a moment that seemed to last forever.

'Well...' the woman said. 'You're quite a find, aren't you?'

Jason rolled off Cynthia's body, his cock and balls soaked with her juices. He watched as the woman licked the fingers that had held them, making an exaggerated slurping noise as she did so, indicating her enjoyment.

He looked around the room. He was surrounded by sex. On each of the brightly lit beds every form of sexual activity was taking place – sucking, fucking, women with their legs spread, kneeling, standing, bending over, cocks inserted in every orifice, breasts licked or pinched or squeezed. This was what this room was for, of course. Everywhere any of the participants looked, they could see others doing what they were doing, adding voyeurism and exhibitionism to their other pleasures, the effect of seeing and being seen a powerful extra stimulus. Jason was aware of it too, aware of the effect it was having on him. It was making him high, like a drug, making his cock throb, making him want more.

The woman in the grey hood had the same idea. She was smiling at him, a strange crooked smile, the scarlet slit of her mouth in stark contrast to the featureless grey of the mask that clung to her face.

She lay on the bed next to Cynthia, arching her sex off the bed, aiming at him. He knew what she wanted and he wanted it too, his need increased by everything that was going on around him. He brought his mouth down to her thigh and kissed the flesh just above the red welt of the stocking, licking and nipping the creamy soft skin. He worked his mouth up, along the taut red suspender to the crease of her pelvis, following it all the way up to her hip, then down again, down to the short pubic hair on the perfect triangle of her belly. Though the hairs looked stubbly they were, in fact, perfectly soft. He licked down to her labia, parting them with the fingers of one hand until he could see the pink nodule of her clitoris.

'Oh, yes . . .' she exclaimed, as she felt his hot tongue hard up against the little knot of nerves.

Cynthia began to come round from her explosive orgasm. Seeing the woman laying next to her she came up to her knees, wanting to give pleasure as she had been pleased. She looked down at her, the almost featureless face and flaring eyes, her mouth open, her tongue playing between her lips.

'He's good at that...' Cyn whispered, bending forward to kiss the woman on the mouth as her hands gathered up her big breasts.

Jason moved so he was lying between the woman's legs. Pushing his hands up under her buttocks, he slid his mouth down over her hairless labia to the mouth of her sex, plunging his tongue as deep inside as it would go. Then he used his hands to work her bottom higher so he could get at the puckered hole of her anus and probe his tongue in there too. The moan this produced was muffled on Cynthia's mouth.

Letting her drop back, he renewed his efforts on her clitoris, circling it with the tip of his tongue, round and round in little spirals, until he could feel her whole body heaving and trembling with sensation, her juices running out of her, her stockinged legs splayed open.

She could stand it no longer. She didn't want to come on his mouth. Breaking away from Cynthia, she pulled Jason's hooded head from her crotch.

'I need cock...'

She sat up and kissed him on the mouth, wanting to taste her own juices. She hoovered them up greedily, then licked the material of the mask, licking his chin and his cheeks. Then she rolled over on her stomach and came up on all fours, spreading her knees apart.

'Give it to me...' she said huskily.

For a moment he looked into her sex, open and wet, her labia parted, her sex like a mouth begging for him, pulsing with need.

Putting his hands on her hips, the sides of the

suspender belt under his palms, he pushed his cock up between her legs until he could feel the wetness and heat of her sex nudging against his glans. Her body shuddered at this first touch. But he did not penetrate immediately. He held his cock there teasingly while he looked around the room. On the bed to his left three women were entwined with each other in a circle, joined like a daisy chain, each mouth on the sex of another, their bodies heaving, panting for breath through their mutual desire. In front of him a woman, a young very slender woman with small breasts and even smaller nipples, was standing by one of the single beds, a man taking her from behind while another sat on the bed, his cock buried in his mouth.

The grey-hooded woman wriggled her buttocks against his cock trying to push it into her. He allowed her to achieve aim, trapping his glans inside her but still leaving the rest of his cock outside.

'Please . . .' she begged, looking over her shoulder at him.

'Is this what you want?' he said through gritted teeth, bucking his hips and plunging his whole shaft into her liquid sex.

'Yes . . . yes . . .' she screamed.

Cynthia was watching him, kneeling on the bed. She looked down at her own slender body, then picked up her nipples with the fingers of both hands. He could see her fingernails digging into the corrugated flesh.

His body began to assert its need, no longer content to be controlled by his mind. He began to pump his cock to and fro. The grey-hooded woman felt good, her sex silky and hot, clinging to the length of his cock, seeming to suck it in.

Cynthia opened her hands and used her palms, circling them against her breasts, crushing her nipples into her chest. With one hand she caressed her flat belly, leaving the other to alternate between her tits. She pushed her fingers down into her labia and he heard her moan as they touched her already-sensitised clitoris. As her finger began to rock it up and down, her other hand ran down her back, over her shoulder pert buttocks and up between her legs. He watched as her fingers penetrated her sex effortlessly, riding up on the tide of juices he had created.

Almost unconsciously the tempo of his cock was increasing, reaming into the chasm between the generous pliant arse of the anonymous woman, her flesh slapping against his navel.

'Why don't you let me do that?'

Jason had not noticed him come over. He stood by the side of the bed in a red hood, his body tanned and muscled, his pubic hair as blond as any woman's. He slipped his hand between Cynthia's legs and pushed one finger up alongside hers in the tunnel of her sex, then pulled her hand away and knelt on the bed behind her. Running his arms around her body, he cupped her small breasts in his hands and pushed his erection into her body.

'Mmm...' Cyn moaned, immediately tipping over on to all fours and reaching back between her legs to grab at the stranger's balls.

The blond stranger, his eyes light blue in the slits of the mask, pushed into her. Jason could see his cock sliding in and out of her body. As their faces were so close the two women kissed, squirming their lips against each other, both men feeling the effect this had on their bodies, their sexes pulsing as the circuit between the couples was completed.

As he watched the stranger's long, leisurely strokes, his cock emerging from Cyn's cunt wet and glistening with the mixture of her juices and his own, Jason felt himself losing control. He was surrounded by sex, everywhere he looked the sight and sound and smell of sex, the aroma of expensive perfume and the musky scent of coupling producing a heady concoction. All around him were beautiful women, some naked, some semi-clothed, silks and satins and lace tightly wrapped around perfect limbs, breasts in every size, the strange hoods reducing heads to uniformity, making the bodies, in contrast, so gloriously different.

He felt his spunk pumping into his cock. He felt the woman opening for him, allowing him deeper and deeper. She was a stranger too, a woman he would fuck but never be able to recognise. There was something exciting about that, about her anonymity and the casualness of it all.

The blond man was increasing his tempo in Cynthia, who was looking up at Jason and smiling. He could read the expression in her eyes. 'Didn't I tell you you'd enjoy it?' they said. She was right. He didn't care about anything else. He had abandoned himself like a satyr, only interested in sex.

He felt the woman contract around him, saw her body tremble. She brought her head up to look at Cynthia and at the woman on the next bed being fucked and giving head at the same time. She was coming, coming fast, her orgasm breaking over the hard cock impaled inside her, so much provocation all around her.

Jason felt her come, felt her body go rigid. His movement stopped, her cunt suddenly holding him like a vice. Then it went slack and he was free again, free to pump faster and harder, watching Cynthia's eyes close, knowing she was coming too. Then he could see nothing, only feel. All the images, all the sights, all the stimuli in the room combined, and his spunk lashed out of his cock into the woman's warm silky welcoming cunt, his senses propelled to heights he could never have imagined.

Chapter Ten

Cynthia poured him a brandy and he took it gratefully. He definitely needed a drink.

'Where are they?'

They had come up in the lift from the cellars, leaving their clothes behind in the changing room, showering first and abandoning the hoods. Jason was now wrapped in a white towelling robe and Cynthia wore a black silk kimono that made her rather pasty complexion look even whiter. The sitting room was deserted.

'They may have gone for a swim. It's warm outside,' Cynthia suggested, knowing full well they hadn't.

'Let's go and look,' Jason said, knocking back the brandy.

They walked through the long corridors of the castle and out into the gardens. The desert air was balmy and dry and the sky above was so clear stars could be seen almost to the horizon – more stars than Jason had ever seen, as though the dark blue canvas of the sky had been covered with a thousand million pinpricks through which a bright light shone from behind.

The water of the pool, lit by floodlights from the sides, was a bright azure blue. Two women, both naked, swam lazily side by side. A man was sitting with his feet dangling in the water watching them. There was no sign of Harry or Nancy.

Cynthia knew where they were of course. She knew

Harriet well enough. She had seen the look in her eyes when she'd first met Nancy at the museum. There was no mistaking it. There had been women she'd lusted after like this before and there would be again. Cynthia knew better than to object. So far Harriet had always come back to her. Perhaps one day it would be different, but Cynthia knew most women might put up with Harriet once or twice but, even with all her wealth and power, no longer. She was too hard, too demanding, too determined to get what she wanted. Cynthia had been treated badly all her life; to her, Harriet's demands were no worse than some of the men she had turned tricks with for a ten-thousandth less than Harriet provided.

She'd done her job. She'd kept Jason busy. They had had enough time alone.

'Come on,' she said. 'They're probably upstairs.'

'Upstairs where?'

'In bed, Jason. You saw the way Harriet was looking at her.'

'I don't think Nancy would . . .' He hesitated.

'Would do it with Harry? Is that what you were going to say?'

He didn't know what Nancy was capable of.

'Harry can be very persuasive. Let's go see.'

She led him through the castle again, its air conditioning welcome after the heat outside. They mounted the marble staircase, their bare feet cold on the stone, and Cynthia took him past the bedroom they had been given, down the corridor – its wall decorated with a collection of Chagall lithographs – and up to two double doors, wider than any of the other doors along the way.

'I expect they're in here,' she said, turning to go back down the hall.

'Aren't you coming in?'

'No... You go in.' She opened the door, leaving it ajar. She knew Harriet wouldn't want her there, wouldn't want to see her again till morning. Blowing Jason a kiss, she walked off down the corridor.

Puzzled, Jason felt a little like a fly walking into the web of a spider. He pushed the door open and tentatively walked inside, closing it behind him. The room beyond was a large sitting room with two sofas and several armchairs arranged around a rectangular coffee table. There was a large picture window overlooking the gardens and the pool. There was a desk in one corner with papers strewn over it, a telephone and a fax machine on a console nearby. On the coffee table was a bottle of champagne in a silver wine cooler and two crystal flutes still half full of wine. Nancy's flame-red dress was draped over one of the chairs. On the far side of the room was another set of double doors, and one of them was slightly ajar...

'More champagne?'

'No thank you.'

'Why don't you take your dress off? I'd like to see your body.'

'Do you always get what you want?'

'Invariably. It goes with the territory.'

'And you want to see my body?'

'Yes. I want to see your tits and your cunt.' Harriet used the words deliberately, wanting to be crude.

Nancy got to her feet, unbuttoned the catch at the back of the halter and let it fall to her waist. She had

had a lot to drink but she didn't think that was affecting her judgement. She liked Harriet. She felt happy with her. She had charmed her like a man, made her feel important and beautiful and, most strangely of all, had made her feel sexy. She looked down at her breasts.

'Is that what you wanted?'

'I want more . . .' Harriet said steadily.

Nancy unzipped the side of the dress and let it drop to the floor. She stepped out of it and picked it up, hanging it over the back of one of the chairs.

'What else do you want?'

'You know.'

'You want to fuck me?'

'Yes.'

Nancy laughed at the idea. It was ridiculous. 'You can't do that!'

'I know,' Harry said quietly with a tone of sadness. 'But it amuses me to try.'

'Come on then. Or are we going to do it in here?'

Harriet got to her feet and opened one of the inner double doors. It lead to a spacious bedroom. A large double bed stood against the far wall, an ornate head- and footboard in scrolled French walnut, its counterpane already neatly folded back.

Nancy stood at the foot of the bed, her long legs sheathed in ultra-sheer nylon tights, her sex covered by a small triangle of black silk, her high heels shaping her calves and the tuck of her buttocks, the drink making her brave. As Harriet sat on the bed, she jumped on it energetically, wrapping her arms around Harriet's neck and kissing her boldly on the mouth, feeling inside her dinner jacket for her tits.

Just as quickly she bounced off the bed again, pulled the tights and panties down together and kicked off her shoes.

'Is this what you wanted to see?' she said, throwing herself back on the bed and opening her legs. 'I've got a lot of hair, haven't I?' she said, combing her pubic curls with her fingers.

'Yes, you have.'

Harriet stood up and stripped off her jacket.

'Have you been with a woman before?' Harriet asked looking at Nancy's naked body.

'Only one.'

'One?'

'Camilla Potts. You know her. Everyone knows her.'

'You've had Camilla?'

'Aren't I lucky? She's very good. Are you as good as that?'

'We'll have to see.'

Harriet stripped away the rest of her outer clothes. She wore a tight-fitting tan-coloured body stocking that in the dim light of the bedroom was difficult to see.

'No tits, no pubis,' Nancy said, mistaking the material for skin.

'You've got wonderful tits...'

Nancy found this very funny and giggled. 'What do you want me to do now?'

'Trust me,' Harriet said quietly. 'Give me your hand.'

'Is that all you want? Just my hand?' She found that very funny too.

'Give me your hand, Nancy,' Harriet said patiently.

Nancy held out her hand. Harriet took it and pulled it up over her head and out towards the corner of the bed. There was a cord there, a silky rope, and she wound it round Nancy's wrist.

'Now the other one...'

'You're tying me up.'

'Does that excite you?'

'Ummm... I'll think about it.'

The ankles followed the wrists, spread-eagling Nancy's willing body across the bed.

'How does that feel?'

Nancy squirmed again the bonds. 'Sexy. It feels sexy.'

'Good.'

Harriet walked over to a door at the side of the bed. It led to the bathroom.

'Where are you going, don't leave me...'

'I'm not leaving you.'

'I want to play with myself.'

'You can't.'

'I know. I want to. Do it for me.'

'Just give me a minute.'

Harriet disappeared into the bathroom.

Nancy felt as if her whole body was humming. Her mind was unable to think of anything, to form any sort of thought that was not involved with the way her sex felt. It felt more alive than it had ever been, like a thing possessed, begging her, pleading with her to be touched, her clitoris squirming under the hood of her labia. She tried to press her thighs together to give it the attention it desperately needed but her legs were tied too far apart and there was no play in the ropes that held her. She raised her head off the bed and looked down at her naked body. The sight made her shudder with pleasure, her big breasts quivering. She was so exposed, so vulnerable.

'You're beautiful, aren't you?' Harriet stood in the bathroom doorway, out of Nancy's line of sight.

'Yes. Yes I am.'

'Do you want to be fucked?'

'Yes. I need it. I need it badly.'

'What's your boyfriend doing now? Would you like to see?'

'No.'

'What would you like?'

Nancy twisted her head round but could still not see Harry. 'I told you.'

Harriet dimmed the lights even lower. She didn't want Nancy to see her. She was ugly like this, it was not how she was meant to be. She sat on the edge of the bed.

'I'm going to give you a very good time.'

'Yes ... please ...'

Harriet stroked Nancy's thigh. She dipped her head to kiss her nipple. Nancy could not see her properly. She was naked she thought, but it was too much effort to strain to see.

Harriet's hand found her labia, parting it to get at her clitoris. Nancy sighed. At least she had what she needed. She wriggled against Harry's finger.

'You'll make me come.'

'I want you to come.'

The finger circled the little knot of nerves.

'Oh, so good ...'

Nancy's feelings were stretched as tautly as her body. There was something about letting herself go like this, giving herself, exposing herself, allowing herself to be taken, being dependent on Harriet's whims, that had turned on a switch in her body she never knew existed.

Harriet was in no hurry. She made Nancy come once on her fingers, then started again more slowly. She made her come by kneading her breasts and again by kneeling between her legs and holding her thigh hard against her sex. She made her come by licking her clitoris. She made her come over and over again. Each climax was harder and deeper. She watched her body shake and tremble, her head tossed from side to side, her arms and legs fighting the silken bonds, no longer the mistress of her own feelings, but loving every minute.

She never penetrated her though, not once. She was leaving that till last.

With Nancy soaked in sweat from the effort of so much excitement, her sex open and as liquid as it would ever be, that time was coming.

Harriet got to her knees. Nancy raised her head, trying to see what she was doing. There was something between Harriet's legs.

'Don't look,' Harriet said.

The dildo was strapped to her loins, its head crafted like a glans, a perfect acorn of imitation flesh, sticking up from between her legs just like a real cock would, its base flared out and beautifully shaped to part the hood of her labia, so every time she pushed it forward little ridges pressed deliciously against her own clitoris. With her hand, she guided the head between the damp soft lips of Nancy's sex and heard her moan at the contact.

'Fuck me,' Nancy said loudly.

She was perfect. So malleable. So feminine. Harriet pushed the dildo home by bucking her hips.

'Oh, yes . . .'

RETURN TO THE CASTING COUCH

Harriet began pounding into her. She had intended to be more subtle, but now she was carried away by Nancy's cries. As the dildo pushed into Nancy's sex, it pushed against her own clitoris. Harder and harder she reamed it in, and harder and harder the feelings from her clitoris became.

'Fuck me, fuck me, fuck me,' Nancy screamed struggling against her bonds, worming down on the dildo buried inside her.

It was as though she was a man, as though she had a cock, as though she really were fucking this beautiful woman. She thought she could feel Nancy's cunt convulsing around the shaft, using it, milking it. She knew Nancy was coming again, but this time she was coming too. She grabbed at Nancy's big tits holding on to them hard, using them to lever herself up more, to push deeper into Nancy and against herself.

Suddenly the room was flooded with light...

Jason pushed the bedroom door open. A wedge of light from the well-lit sitting room spilled into the glow illuminating the bed. For a long second Jason stood trying to make sense of what he saw, the masculine figure of Harriet hunched over the prone Nancy, as though she were fucking her, tight black leather straps girding her buttocks and waist.

He could see the cords around Nancy's wrists and ankles, could see she was tied helplessly to the bed, just as Hanna Silverstein had tied him, just as he'd been tied in *Escape of the Whores*. But Nancy was struggling.

'Get off her...' Jason shouted.

Harriet did nothing, did not look around, did not stop pumping her hips.

'Get off her.'

Jason strode over to the bed and grabbed at Harriet's shoulders, trying to pull her off.

'No...' Nancy cried through the fog of her feelings, suddenly realising what was happening. 'No... don't...'

'Get off her,' Jason shouted, mistaking Nancy's words for distress. He tried to wrestle Harriet off but she clung tenaciously, still pumping her hips, finding Jason's presence and behaviour exciting, propelling her nearer and nearer to orgasm.

'No...' Nancy was so close to coming herself she couldn't bear the thought of having the long dildo torn from her body.

Unable to get the leverage he needed standing over the bed, Jason jumped up on to it, getting behind Harriet, kneeling between her legs, trying to pull her arms away from Nancy's body. Harriet struggled back.

'Get off me.'

The belt of the towelling robe came free. Despite his anger, or perhaps because of it, Jason had an erection and wrestling with Harriet was making it harder. He managed to pull one of her arms away from Nancy.

'No...' Nancy tried to gather her thoughts, tried to find the words to stop Jason. 'Stop it, stop it,' she said. But this only made it worse, making him redouble his efforts.

'Jason... I want it. I want it...'

'What?'

'Leave her alone.'

Jason stopped, letting Harriet go. Without impediment, she started pumping into Nancy again, harder than before, her buttocks pushing into Jason's cock.

With part of his mind, Jason knew he should climb off the bed and let them get on with it, but he was not using that part of his mind. He was thinking with his cock, if that could be called thinking. Following his instinct – instincts honed and sharpened by all his experiences in the last few weeks – he pushed his cock up between Harriet's legs.

'No!' she cried.

'Yes,' he insisted.

But Harriet did not stop moving. She continued plunging the dildo into Nancy's sex, groping for her tits again, just as Jason was groping for hers.

'No . . .' she repeated, but less insistently, as his fingers found the barely discernible mounds of her breasts and pinched her tiny nipples.

Jason was looking down at Nancy, her body spread-eagled, her arms and legs stretched taut, the silky ropes wrapped round her wrists and ankles. He remembered how he'd felt, what it was like to be spread and helpless, unable to do anything but feel. His cock pulsed at the memory and slipped between the lips of Harriet's sex. Bucking his hips he pushed right up into her, not caring about anything any more, not thinking this might spoil everything, his plans, his career, only listening to his need.

'No!' Harriet screamed.

Jason reamed forward, pushing up into her, his movement pushing the dildo forward too, deeper into Nancy and harder against Harriet's clit.

'Yes,' he cried triumphantly. For once he didn't feel as if he was being used. He felt as if he was in control of his own destiny, pistoning into Harriet's sex where no man had been before, in and out, forcing the dildo in and out too, bringing himself off, feeling his spunk rising, needing to get it out.

'God, god, god . . .' Harriet moaned. He could not tell whether the words were disgust or pleasure.

'Jason . . . Jason . . .' Nancy panted, orgasm overtaking her, the extraordinary feeling of being spread and splayed, tied and stretched, with her sex on fire, rocketing her to climax. She struggled desperately against her bonds, for no reason other than to feel them and the effect they produced in her.

Jason saw her come, saw her eyes roll back, her muscles pull one last time on the ropes and then go slack. He was on the brink himself. He could feel the base of the dildo, slick and wet against his balls, could feel Harriet's hard buttocks on his navel, and her sex clinging to his cock. He pushed forward one final time and, almost before he'd stopped, his spunk jetted out, his cock kicking and jerking in the confines of her sex.

Unexpectedly, he felt Harriet's whole body convulse, arching back up from Nancy, pushing into him with almost manic power, then locking, bent like a bow.

'God . . .' the word came from the depths of her body. This time there was no mistaking its meaning. The words was hoarse with pleasure, a low animal noise that came from the very soul where profound sensation had stirred, for the first time, a nerve that had lain dormant for so long . . .

Chapter Eleven

There was a slight breeze from the west, pleasantly cooling the hot desert air which, even at ten in the morning, was more than welcome.

A table had been laid on a small terrace overlooking the gardens, where sprinklers were spraying in great circles of misty droplets trying to keep the greenery green against the scorching sun. A white canvas parasol shaded the table where Cynthia and Harriet both sat in silk robes, Cynthia's baby pink, Harriet's a polka-dotted dark blue.

'Good morning,' Harry said brightly, as Jason and Nancy were led up to the table by the servant she had sent to request the pleasure of their company at breakfast. Harriet got to her feet, took Nancy's hand and kissed it, drawing out one of the chairs by the table for her to sit on with elaborate politeness, while the servant did the same for Jason.

From the helicopter pad they could hear the rotor engines increasing in power and, just as they sat down, the plane hovered into view then turned to the west and flew away.

There was a telephone on the table which rang as the waiter poured coffee. Harriet answered it. She said 'yes' twice in rapid succession then replaced the handset.

'Please forgive me,' she said. 'What would you like for breakfast?'

The activities of the previous night had left Jason feeling ravenously hungry and, having taken to the American tradition, he ordered ham and eggs over easy, home fries and pancakes with maple syrup. Nancy, no less hungry, had the same.

'I'm starving,' he explained.

'I'm sure,' Harriet said. 'Now, Jason, I wanted to start the day on the right note. I should have explained all this to you yesterday when you arrived...'

Cold fingers gripped Jason's stomach. It sounded like the beginning of an excuse. He looked over at Nancy.

'... but then I got caught up in something else.'

'Of course,' he said graciously, feeling anything but.

'So we should talk about it now, the script I mean, the Len Furey film...'

Did she say that with a definite sneer?

'Well... How can I put this? I think it's great. It's funny, exciting, commercial. Very commercial. What's more, it's perfect for you, just perfect. You're exactly the right actor to play it.'

Jason felt himself grinning from ear to ear. He tried to look sophisticated and cool, crossing his legs and leaning back in the chair, smoothing his mouth into a small tight smile, but the grin sneaked back after a minute or two.

'I've sent the helicopter to get Len Furey. We'll go through all the details over lunch but I want to do this picture. The lawyers are already here. We'll do a deal, I promise you.'

Harriet covered Jason's hand with her own.

'That's great.'

'You'll be a star,' Cyn said excitedly.

'I should say so,' Harriet agreed. 'If we get a move

on we can start shooting in two months. I want the picture out for the Christmas season. It's going to be big.'

'I think so,' was all Jason could think to say.

The waiter arrived with a tray of food, setting the plates down in front of Nancy and Jason, who found his appetite had suddenly disappeared.

'There is just one thing you can do for me in return,' Harriet said, looking straight into Jason's blue eyes.

'Anything,' Jason said and meant it.

'How shall I put this . . . Let's say I've always enjoyed surprises. When you are as wealthy as I am, surprises are difficult to find. You surprised me last night, Jason. You surprised me wonderfully.'

'I didn't mean to . . .'

'Shh . . .' Harriet smiled. Smiling wasn't a natural thing for her to do and it creased her chubby face in unaccustomed places. 'It wasn't a criticism. I would like you to surprise me again, that's all. I'd like to think, with us working together on this film, we would be able to find the opportunities for you to surprise me quite often. That would be nice, wouldn't it?'

'Yes, yes . . .' Jason's mind was racing.

'Sometimes we could get together, all four of us. Sometimes when I'm really in the mood to be astonished, just you and I, Jason . . .' She said it quietly, her face softening, her body language the most feminine Jason had ever seen from her. 'Would you do that for me?'

'Yes.'

He wanted to say a lot of other things but what was the point? This was Hollywood. There was no such thing as a free lunch, let alone the free financing of a major feature film. If his months in Hollywood had taught him nothing else, it had taught him that.

'Yes,' he repeated firmly almost to himself, 'that would be great.'

'Jason, come in . . . come in . . .'

Hanna Silverstein was wearing her usual white – a white sweater and skirt, with a big gold brooch pinned on the wool just above her breast. Just as usual her hands and wrists were bejewelled with gold. She kissed both his cheeks, her bony fingers cupping his face.

'So nice to see you. Champagne?'

'That would be nice.'

She walked him through to the terrace where a bottle of champagne and two glasses stood on one of the white tables. She poured.

'Cheers,' he said.

'Cheers.'

He looked at the swimming pool and the sloping lawns. A small tractor was working its way up and down, leaving wide swathes of mown and flattened grass behind it. The sun was shining brightly and the flowers planted in terracotta tubs were a riot of colour.

'So the news is all good?' Hanna said, sitting down and beckoning him to do the same.

'Yes . . .' he thought she meant the news about the Len Furey film. News travels fast in tinsel town.

'I told you I was going to make it up to you, didn't I?'

'You've told me a lot of things, Hanna. Not all of them true.'

'You're right. I told you that. I even apologised didn't I?'

'Yes.' He didn't say 'but', though it was in the tone of his voice.

'Well, I've been thinking. I mean I brought you here, all the way here, to play the lead in *The Casting Couch*.'

Jason knew what was coming. For once he had the advantage over Hanna Silverstein. It was nice to see her squirming for a change.

'It just seemed ridiculous to me. I mean, you're so right for the part. I always said that, didn't I? I spent a lot of money bringing you over here . . .'

'But the part's cast, Hanna. You said yourself. Al Prentiss . . .'

'Al Prentiss isn't right, Jason. He hasn't got your qualities.'

'Really?'

'I want you back in the lead.'

'Really?' He didn't sound surprised.

'I've told Al he's out. That's it. When I make a decision it stays made.'

'You decided to cast Al,' he taunted.

'No, Jason, that was forced on me. Now I've made my mind up to cast you.'

Jason said nothing. Nor did he smile.

'Aren't you pleased?'

'Yes, I'm pleased.' Another unspoken 'but'.

'So come over here and give me a big hug.'

'I don't think so.'

'Jason, Jason. I still want you, baby. All those great times we had in bed. I've apologised. I've got you the lead again. Aren't we going to be friends and kiss and make up?'

'Hanna, you're having me back in *The Casting Couch* because Bill Talbot found out Al Prentiss was starring in a rather nasty gay film and told you he was out. It's nothing to do with me or with us. I'll do the movie for you, I'd be crazy not to, but first I'm doing a film for Len Furey financed by Harriet Teitelbaum.'

'Hey, that's wonderful.' She looked so surprised she obviously hadn't heard.

'You didn't know?'

'It's great news.'

'So *The Casting Couch* will have to wait.'

'That's no problem.'

'Good.'

'So now come and give me a big kiss.'

'I don't think so. You've screwed me once, Hanna. I don't think I want to be screwed again.'

'Jason, Jesus, I thought . . .'

'I had a good time? I did. I had a good time but you used me and you know you did. You admitted it. You're not going to get the chance again.'

'Not once for old times' sake?' she said in her little girl's voice.

'No.'

Hanna got up and came to rest against the arm of his chair. 'Jason, I need you.' She touched his cheek. Suddenly the look appeared in her face, the look he had seen after her early morning swims, the look of the child, of innocence, of care. 'I need you . . . don't be cruel to me . . .'

She ran her hand down his neck into his open shirt. Her fingers started undoing the top button. He caught her hand by the wrist.

'No,' he said firmly.

She twisted round and kissed him on the mouth. 'Take me, Jason,' she whispered in his ear, her breath hot, her hand struggling to escape, breaking his grip and snaking down into his lap.

She got to her feet again and walked into the house. He followed her, hearing her shoes clacking on the stairs. He got as far as the front door. One more time wouldn't hurt would it? That wouldn't compromise his principles. Next time he'd say no. One last time for all the good times Hanna had given him. After all, without her he'd never have come to Hollywood in the first place.

He turned and started up the stairs . . .

'You love it, don't you?'

'Yes, I love it.'

'You little bitch. You kinky little bitch.'

Camilla Potts was almost naked, her firm rip sensuous body clothed in a pair of black hold-up stockings, their welts made from thick black lace, and black high heels. She stood by the bed her arms akimbo, her legs apart, the hairless labia of her sex already glistening with excitement.

She ran hand over Nancy's fleshy arse. Nancy gasped. The four strokes of the strap had reddened it and it radiated heat.

'More?'

'Yes, oh yes . . .' Nancy begged passionately, her body alive, currents of sensation coursing through her like electricity.

She was tied to the brass bedstead of her bed by silk scarves, spread-eagled as she had been at Harry's, wanting to feel that sensation again, her limbs powerless, her centre, the centre of her sex, melting and molten.

'Like this?' Camilla brought the strap down hard, the sound of leather on pliant flesh filling the small room.

'Yes,' Nancy screamed, the pain as close to pleasure as to be indistinguishable.

'You little bitch,' Camilla repeated bringing the leather strap down for a sixth time.

'Yes, I am, I am...' Nancy moaned, writhing, her big breasts against the sheet, her hard nipples pressed against her chest. She tried to push her clitoris against the mattress too. She was going to come. Camilla dropped the strap and worked her hand down between Nancy's navel and the bed, combing through her hairy belly until she found her clitoris.

'Oh, oh...' Nancy screamed.

Camilla circled it with her finger, then rocked it to and fro, not at all gently. Nancy struggled against her bonds. Camilla inserted one finger, then two, into her sex, as far as they would go.

'Yes, yes...' was Nancy's response, her eyes tight shut as she rocked her body against the silk that held her so tightly in time to the tempo Camilla used to plough into her body. 'Oh yes...' she screamed, as she lost control and cascaded down into an abyss of pleasure, wallowing in it, the tautness of her muscles in her limbs in such contrast to the soft malleability of her sex against Camilla's fingers.

'So, we're celebrating, are we?' Jason said, standing in the bedroom door. Camilla hadn't heard the news about Len Furey's film – which had a good straight part for her – until Nancy had told her.

'You bet,' she said.

'Can anyone join in or is this a private party?'

'Very private,' Camilla said.

'Fuck her, Jason. I want to watch you fuck her,' Nancy said opening her eyes and feeling her senses return.

Camilla went over to the video and turned it on. The screen lit up with a massive close-up of Jason's cock. It was plunging in and out of Camilla's hairless sex, while her manicured and red-varnished fingernails toyed with her clitoris.

'Yes, like that,' Nancy said twisting her head round to see.

On screen, Camilla was bent over a bed. Jason was standing behind her, his jeans around his knees. Camilla bent over Nancy's bed and pushed her buttocks out. The black lace welts of the stockings almost touched the tuck where her bottom met her thigh.

Jason pushed his jeans down to his knees. His cock sprung up expectantly.

'Yes,' Camilla said wriggling her bum.

Nancy turned her head to the other side. Camilla's sex was only inches away. She saw Jason's cock, red and erect, approaching the furrow of Camilla's labia.

He would have liked to free Nancy so she could use her mouth on Camilla's clit and her hands on his balls but there wasn't time. They would do that later. For the moment he needed to push his cock into the tight wet silky tunnel of Camilla's sex and feel again how it sucked him in, clung to him, how it seemed to massage the great sword of flesh as he ploughed into her.

He looked down at Camillas's long slender thighs, the welts of the stockings dimpling the flesh. He looked down at Nancy stretched and spread, the lush bush of hair between her legs sticking out from the base of her buttocks. He looked at the television screen and watched as his cock reamed into the same body he was penetrating now.

He let his feelings flood through him as his cock slid into Camilla's sex. But he felt something new, something he'd not felt before. He'd used his body and let it be used. He'd fucked some beautiful women and enjoyed every minute of it. He'd had sexual experiences that defied his wildest fantasies. He'd hated Hollywood for using him but now, for the first time, it was dawning on him that he had done it. He had got what he wanted – he'd played the system and won. Looking down at the two women in front of him, his victory seemed unbelievably sweet.

More Erotic Fiction from Headline Delta

EROS IN SUMMER

Anonymous

In summer, so they say, as the temperature rises so does one's ardour. This couldn't be more true of the virile Sir Andrew Nelham and his nubile cousin Sophia. Andy tastes the pleasures of the Sussex seaside towns while on business – and pleasure *is* his business – as Sophia relaxes in Brighton after an arduous winter.

Sophia, open and amorous as ever, finds no shortage of holiday companions to play with, while Andy discovers that the tourist attractions are by no means limited to the sights. From the intriguing and tantalising temptations of Parson Darby's Cave to the sumptuous titbits offered at Arundel Castle by a delectable proprietress – served under rather than over the table – Andy's experiences satisfy all appetites. Their seaside jaunt climaxes in a party at the select and somewhat outré Fitz Club, where they celebrate their new summer friendships in the most delightful way...

Look out for the many other arousing adventures in the EROS series:
EROS IN THE COUNTRY   EROS IN TOWN
EROS ON THE GRAND TOUR   EROS IN THE NEW WORLD
EROS IN THE FAR EAST   THE EROS COLLECTION
EROS IN HIGH PLACES   EROS IN SOCIETY
EROS OFF THE RAILS   THE ULTIMATE EROS COLLECTION
EROS STRIKES GOLD   EROS IN SPRINGTIME

FICTION/EROTICA   0 7472 4463 4

Headline Delta Erotic Survey

In order to provide the kind of books you like to read - and to qualify for a free erotic novel of the Editor's choice - we would appreciate it if you would complete the following survey and send your answers, together with any further comments, to:

> Headline Book Publishing
> FREEPOST (WD 4984)
> London
> NW1 0YR

1. Are you male or female?
2. Age? Under 20 / 20 to 30 / 30 to 40 / 40 to 50 / 50 to 60 / 60 to 70 / over
3. At what age did you leave full-time education?
4. Where do you live? (Main geographical area)
5. Are you a regular erotic book buyer / a regular book buyer in general / both?
6. How much approximately do you spend a year on erotic books / on books in general?
7. How did you come by this book?
7a. If you bought it, did you purchase from: a national bookchain / a high street store / a newsagent / a motorway station / an airport / a railway station / other........
8. Do you find erotic books easy / hard to come by?
8a. Do you find Headline Delta erotic books easy / hard to come by?
9. Which are the best / worst erotic books you have ever read?
9a. Which are the best / worst Headline Delta erotic books you have ever read?
10. Within the erotic genre there are many periods, subjects and literary styles. Which of the following do you prefer:
10a. (period) historical / Victorian / C20th / contemporary / future?
10b. (subject) nuns / whores & whorehouses / Continental frolics / s&m / vampires / modern realism / escapist fantasy / science fiction?

10c. (styles) hardboiled / humorous / hardcore / ironic / romantic / realistic?
10d. Are there any other ingredients that particularly appeal to you?
11. We try to create a cover appearance that is suitable for each title. Do you consider them to be successful?
12. Would you prefer them to be less explicit / more explicit?
13. We would be interested to hear of your other reading habits. What other types of books do you read?
14. Who are your favourite authors?
15. Which newspapers do you read?
16. Which magazines?
17. Do you have any other comments or suggestions to make?

If you would like to receive a free erotic novel of the Editor's choice (available only to UK residents), together with an up-to-date listing of Headline Delta titles, please supply your name and address. Please allow 28 days for delivery.

Name..

Address..

....

....

A selection of Erotica from Headline

SCANDAL IN PARADISE	Anonymous	£4.99 ☐
UNDER ORDERS	Nick Aymes	£4.99 ☐
RECKLESS LIAISONS	Anonymous	£4.99 ☐
GROUPIES II	Johnny Angelo	£4.99 ☐
TOTAL ABANDON	Anonymous	£4.99 ☐
AMOUR ENCORE	Marie-Claire Villefranche	£4.99 ☐
COMPULSION	Maria Caprio	£4.99 ☐
INDECENT	Felice Ash	£4.99 ☐
AMATEUR DAYS	Becky Bell	£4.99 ☐
EROS IN SPRINGTIME	Anonymous	£4.99 ☐
GOOD VIBRATIONS	Jeff Charles	£4.99 ☐
CITIZEN JULIETTE	Louise Aragon	£4.99 ☐

All Headline books are available at your local bookshop or newsagent, or can be ordered direct from the publisher. Just tick the titles you want and fill in the form below. Prices and availability subject to change without notice.

Headline Book Publishing, Cash Sales Department, Bookpoint, 39 Milton Park, Abingdon, OXON, OX14 4TD, UK. If you have a credit card you may order by telephone – 0235 400400.

Please enclose a cheque or postal order made payable to Bookpoint Ltd to the value of the cover price and allow the following for postage and packing:
UK & BFPO: £1.00 for the first book, 50p for the second book and 30p for each additional book ordered up to a maximum charge of £3.00.
OVERSEAS & EIRE: £2.00 for the first book, £1.00 for the second book and 50p for each additional book.

Name ....

Address ....

....

....

If you would prefer to pay by credit card, please complete:
Please debit my Visa/Access/Diner's Card/American Express (delete as applicable) card no:

Signature .... Expiry Date ....